TriQuarterly

TriQuarterly is

an international

journal of

writing, art and

cultural inquiry

published at

Northwestern

University

TriQuarterly

issue 128

Editor
Susan Firestone Hahn

Associate Editor
Ian Morris

Operations Coordinator
Kirstie Felland

Cover Design
Gini Kondziolka

Editorial Assistant
Amy Levine

Assistant Editor
Joanne Diaz

TriQuarterly Fellow
Brent Mix

Contributing Editors
John Barth
Lydia R. Diamond
Rita Dove
Stuart Dybek
Richard Ford
Sandra M. Gilbert
Robert Hass
Edward Hirsch
Li-Young Lee
Lorrie Moore
Alicia Ostriker
Carl Phillips
Robert Pinsky
Susan Stewart
Mark Strand
Alan Williamson

TriQuarterly is pleased to announce:

Carolyn Alessio has won an Illinois Arts Council award for her story "Mijo" (125),

Beth Ann Fennelly's poem "Why We Shouldn't Write Love Poems, or If We Must, Why We Shouldn't Publish Them" (115) has been selected by editor David Lehman to appear in *The Best American Erotic Poetry: From 1800 to the Present* (Scribner, 2008),

ArLynn Leiber Presser has won an Illinois Arts Council award for her essay "The Ghost Light" (124),

Phillip Robertson's essay "In the Mosque of the Imam Ali" (123) will appear in the *Best American Essays 2007* (Houghton Mifflin), edited by David Foster Wallace.

Contents

Editors of this Issue
Barbara Hamby and David Kirby

Cover: Photo by Barbara Hamby

Barbara Hamby and David Kirby

Pleasure First

Grown-up readers apply the same test to literature that kindergartners do, says Auden; the only question worth asking of a poem or story or play is, do I like it? As adults, often we take up a book because someone tells us to or we think we should or we believe it might benefit us in some way. Originally, though, we all came to poetry though pleasure. This issue of *TriQuarterly* consists of poems that give its editors a heightened pleasure, one that can be accounted for at least partially in this introduction.

The phrase "ultra-talk" first appeared in a 2002 essay called "Gabfest" by Mark Halliday about David Kirby's collection *The House of Blue Light*. There Halliday defines the ultra-talk poem as one in which detailed anecdotes, bits of pop culture past and present, and references to books read, are woven together, as though the poet is saying, "'These seven or eleven things are swirling in my head and I feel an emotional circuit among them and this poem is trying to light up the whole circuit.'" To Halliday, this type of poetry is hyperjunctive rather than disjunctive (like Ashbery's, say); he calls Kirby's "an anti-leap aesthetic" but says "if he does hop occasionally, he announces it loudly and makes sure you hop alongside him without spilling your drink."

A few years after "Gabfest" appeared, David Graham published an essay called "The Ultra-Talk Poem and Mark Halliday," where he extends the phrase to the work of Denise Duhamel, David Clewell, Albert Goldbarth, Barbara Hamby, and, mainly, that of Halliday himself. Graham also gives his own definition of ultra-talk poetry, calling it "garrulous to an extreme, quite often self-reflexive, determinedly associative, and frequently humorous."

As "a welcome alternative" to "much current poetry that is oversolemn, willfully opaque, or radically atomized in thought or typography," Graham notes that "ultra-talk poems . . . are typically quite personal in tone without being unaware of the absurdities inherent in a self-presentational aesthetic," though "their ironies seem different in spirit from what has been termed the 'postmodern wink,' that sometimes predictable deployment of language to undercut its own rhetoric, thus denying the reader many of the traditional pleasures of poetry." He concludes: "Many ultra-talk poems are very aware of postmodern theory, and may toy with ideas and techniques absorbed from that realm; but ultimately the emphasis is on the poem as giving pleasure."

Ah, pleasure: your forms are many, yet you are to be experienced, not defined. That hasn't kept the pigeonholers from trying. Before ultra-talk, there was the Maverick Poetry gathered by Steve Kowit in *The Maverick Poets*, a group including Frank Bidart, Stephen Dobyns, Edward Field, Allen Ginsberg, Dorianne Laux, Sharon Olds, and Gary Snyder, a group neither Beat nor academic but one in a "contemporary Whitmanesque idiom," as Kowit notes in his introduction, poets writing "an heroic and colloquial poetry: large-spirited, socially-engaged, heart-centered and defiantly wacky," work not "tepid, mannered and opaque" (that word again).

In *Book Lust*, Nancy Pearl identifies the Kitchen-Sink Poets, a "gang of five" made up of Billy Collins, David Kirby, Campbell McGrath, James Tate, and Dean Young, as the Kitchen-Sink Poets, all of whom share a "conversational, seemingly stream-of-consciousness approach to their subjects (which are wacky in their own right) and the ability to make readers feel that they're about to become involved in often complicated and convoluted stories."

The most notable predecessor to the term "ultra-talk," though, is the Stand Up Poetry collected by Charles Harper Webb in his 1990 and 2002 anthologies and practiced by many of the poets named above as well as Kim Addonizio, Catherine Bowman, Maxine Chernoff, Jim Daniels, Stephen Dunn, Russell Edson, Bob Hicok, Tony Hoagland, Jack Myers, Maureen Seaton, Maura Stanton, Judith Taylor, Natasha Trethewey, and Al Zolynas. Webb uses "Stand Up" in the double sense of both "Stand Up comic" and "Stand Up guy" and then lists the qualities of the Stand Up poem: humor, performability, clarity, natural language, flights of fancy, a strong individual voice, emotional punch, a close relationship to fiction, use of urban and popular culture, and wide-open subject matter.

And whether they acknowledge it or not, all of these essayists and anthologists, including the co-editors of this issue of *TriQuarterly*, owe much to the idea of "leaping poetry" discussed by Robert Bly in his 1975 book in which he describes the wild association and surrealism of such poets as Neruda, Lorca, and Vallejo.

"A Wild Irregular Strain"

By now, the reader with a sense of history will be saying, "What's so new about all of this? Poets have been writing this way for years!" Both Mark Halliday and David Graham would agree with this hypothetical reader. Halliday says that ultra-talk goes back through the poetry of Kenneth Koch and Frank O'Hara to that of Swift and Byron; Graham lists Kenneth Fearing, Paul Blackburn, and A. R. Ammons as recent practitioners and includes Coleridge among ultra-talk's Neoclassical and Romantic forefathers.

Indeed, isn't ultra-talk as old as poetry itself—hasn't some form of it been written, not for years, but for millennia? Before there was Maverick or Kitchen-Sink or Stand Up Poetry or Leaping Poetry, there was dithyrambic poetry; the word "dithyramb," which originally meant "a frenzied, impassioned choric hymn and dance of ancient Greece in honor of Dionysus," has come to mean "a wildly enthusiastic speech or piece of writing" or "poem written in a wild irregular strain." Neither lyric nor narrative, the dithyramb embraces both the emotionalism of the former and the sprawl of the latter.

The greatest poetry in the dithyrambic tradition may be found in Euripides' *Bacchae*, and the six poetical books of the Old Testament (Job, Psalms, Proverbs, Ecclesiastes, Song of Solomon, and Lamentations) stand as a fine example from the Judeo-Christian tradition. It may be no accident that religion and dithyrambs seem closely tied, since dialogue is at the heart of confrontations between mortals and their maker. All journeys to the underworld are dithyrambic in one way or another, as seen in the relevant parts of *The Epic of Gilgamesh*, *The Iliad*, *The Odyssey*, *The Aeneid*, and *The Vision of Tundal*, a twelfth-century account of an Irish knight's trip through Hell.

The master traveler to dark realms is, of course, Dante. Down to hell he goes, not alone but accompanied by *his* master, the Virgil who guided him as Dante guides us, and there he sees every manner of creature: bad popes, virtuous pagans, heroes from legend like Odysseus, three-headed dogs, harpies, centaurs, imps and demons and Satan himself, his beloved Beatrice, angel-headed hipsters, saintly motorcyclists. Yes, it is Ginsberg's *Howl* that is paraphrased at the end of this list, but that is because these two poets would have much to say to each other: they would disagree violently on many matters, and Dante would not have hesitated to put Ginsberg in Circle Seven of his Inferno with the other sodomites, but they would have conversed brilliantly because each had a large mind and loved learning.

"A Foxy and Relentlessly Slippery Flexibility"

Between Dante Alighieri and Allen Ginsberg there are many "wildly enthusiastic speeches or pieces of writing," notably those that occur in the plays of Shakespeare, a master at mixing levels of rhetoric, speaking to both courtiers and groundlings alike when he uses a polysyllabic Latinate word and then "translates" it with a crisp Anglo-Saxon synonym, as in Act II, Scene ii of *Twelfth Night*, when Sir Andrew Aguecheek listens to a song sung by Feste and pronounces his voice "mellifluous" and then, in his next line, "sweet."

Shakespeare was derided for his lack of education by such jealous contemporaries as Robert Greene, who sneered that he was "Maister of Artes in Neither University" (this enmity didn't bother Shakespeare, who cheerfully filched the plot of *The Winter's Tale* from Greene's *Pandosto: The Triumph of Time*). But he possessed a tool greater by far than any a university could give him; he had at his command what Simon Winchester, in his history of the *Oxford English Dictionary*, calls the "foxy and relentlessly slippery flexibility" of the English language.

Camille Paglia writes of growing up in an Italian-speaking community in upstate New York and then falling hard for English, for "what fascinated me about English was what I later recognized as its hybrid etymology: blunt Anglo-Saxon concreteness, sleek Norman French urbanity, and polysyllabic Greco-Roman abstraction. The clash of these elements, as competitive as Italian dialects, is invigorating, richly entertaining, and often funny, as it is to Shakespeare, who gets tremendous effects out of their interplay. The dazzling multiplicity of sounds and word choices in English makes it brilliantly suited to be a language of poetry. . . . The words jostle and provoke one another and mischievously shift their meanings over time."

As with much else in contemporary culture, a huge debt is owed to Shakespeare for using so many now-familiar words for the first time, as when, for example, he added the Norman French *-able* to Old English *laugh* to allow Salanio in *The Merchant of Venice* to declare a jest *laughable*. And the rich stew of English that is compounded largely of the three linguistic traditions that Paglia mentions has been further thickened by words from dozens of other languages, including Malay (*bamboo, ketchup*), Turkish (*kiosk, sofa*), Algonquian (*raccoon, wampum*), and Dutch (*cruise, knapsack*).

Not every *ayatollah* (Persian) or *mullah* (Urdu) is likely to endorse Simon Winchester's chest-thumping description of English as "so vast, so sprawling, so wonderfully unwieldy, so subtle, and now in its never-ending fullness so undeniably magnificent." Yet no one can deny the language's utility to such word-drunk poets as William Blake, whose "Marriage of Heaven and Hell" blends the chatter of devils and angels with the screeches of copulating, cannibalistic monkeys as well as the speaker's mid-journey refutations of Aristotle and Swedenborg.

After Blake, the greatest dithyrambic poets of modern times are Whitman and Ginsberg; H.D. and Anne Waldman are their children, as are, in many ways, such performance artist as Tracie Morris and the poets of the Nuyorican Café. And while this is not the place to explore broader applications, surely Nietzsche and Melville wrote dithyrambic prose, work rich in Bakhtinian heteroglossia; there is much in their work of the "carnivalesque" and "polyvocal," to use terms borrowed from European criticism (or the "riotous" and "many-voiced," as we Anglophones might say). In fact, as evidenced by the work of Mikhail Bakhtin and Camille Paglia themselves, there is even a dithyrambic criticism—indeed, much, perhaps most, of poststructuralist theory might be called dithyrambic.

Throughout the long history of the kind of writing that is described here, one consistent note is that of laughter, a sound heard too seldom in contemporary poetry. That, according to Billy Collins, is "the fault of the Romantics, who eliminated humor from poetry. Shakespeare's hilarious, Chaucer's hilarious. [Then] the Romantics killed off humor, and they also eliminated sex, things which were replaced by landscape. I thought that was a pretty bad trade-off, so I'm trying to write about humor and landscape, and occasionally sex."

A Philosophy of Composition

To add to what Mark Halliday and David Graham have offered by way of definition, this essay will conclude with the co-editors' own list of ultra-talk poetry's most eye-catching features.

Not that every (or, for that matter, any) poet here wrote with these features in mind, at least as they are defined below. But John Maynard Keynes said famously that a person who thinks himself free from intellectual influence is usually "the slave of some defunct economist." (Keynes also said "words ought to be a little wild, for they are the assaults of thoughts on the unthinking.") And from the time of Aristotle and Horace to the present day, every poet has had a poetics, consciously or not. In "The Philosophy of Composition," Poe provides a checklist for everything a good poem needs, and if Poe's formula leaves out such innate qualities as excellence, that doesn't detract from the fact that "The Raven" is a great and talky poem.

Not every ultra-talk poem is going to have the same characteristics. But a philosophy of composition for ultra-talk poets and their readers would include these traits:

1. A poem features the voice of a speaker but other voices as well, at least by implication: the speech of an actor standing alone in a pencil spotlight is made richer by the eloquence of the players who are only temporarily silent.
2. A poem will focus on the present moment but also convey an awareness of a larger world of time and space: a moment is most resonant when it appears to have a past and a future as well as dimensions on every side.
3. A poem that deals in comedy will acknowledge tragedy. And the other way around: the funniest poem will have a dark heart, just as a good sad poem will seem to have been written by a poet capable of laughter.
4. A poem that works on stage will work on the page as well: the best poems are a delight to hear aloud but will also grow richer during a silent rereading.

It's no accident that these characteristics of ultra-talk poetry are expressed as paired opposites, for the ultra-talk poem is willing to include or at least consider everything.

Notes

The Halliday and Graham essays appear respectively as "Gabfest," *Parnassus*, 26 (2002), 203-215 and "The Ultra-Talk Poem & Mark Halliday," *Valparaiso Poetry Review*, 7 (Fall/Winter 2005-2006), online at http://www.valpo.edu/english/vpr/. These four books represent additional attempts to present the kind of poem described in this essay: Robert Bly's *Leaping Poetry: An Idea With Poems and Translations* (Boston: Beacon Press, 1975), Steve Kowit's *The Maverick Poets: An Anthology* (Santee, CA: Gorilla Press, 1988), Nancy Pearl's *Book Lust* (Seattle: Sasquatch Press, 2003), and Charles Harper Webb's *Stand Up Poetry: An Expanded Anthology* (Iowa City: University of Iowa Press, 2002). The definition of "dithyramb" is taken from www.dictionary.com. Simon Winchester's *The Meaning of Everything: The Story of the Oxford English Dictionary* (New York: Oxford University Press, 2004) is the source of the lines on the richness of the English language. As a model of contemporary poetry criticism, it would be hard to find a better example than Camille Paglia's *Break, Blow, Burn* (New York: Pantheon, 2005). More on dithyrambic prose can be found in David Kirby's essay collection *Ultra-Talk: Johnny Cash, The Mafia, Shakespeare, Drum Music, St. Teresa of Avila, and 17 Other Colossal Topics of Conversation* (Athens: University of Georgia Press, 2007); with some changes, passages from several of those essays appear here.

Albert Goldbarth

Channeling the Lord

> She says God talks to her through her TV.
>
> *National Enquirer*

Not surprising—not if the Book and the books are right
about immanence and ubiquity. Then, he would speak to us
through everything. The heart, and the artichoke heart;
the bleeding orange of the sunset as it dawdles
on the laketop, and the mortuary version of that color
in the potted meat as it's tinned in its turn on the can line.
Once there's everything, there is no "bathos." Presupposing
an everything, then "discrepancy" disappears from the dictionary.
The voice in the thickening steam as it issues from a vent
in the dim of the oracle's cave; the voice in the vent,
the bubbling ocean-bottom vent, where ten-foot tube worms extend
and retract and extend in a primal frolic of water so impossibly hot
it would melt a sunken car to dribble. And we needn't be ordained
or on our knees or in a vision-state of shamanic tizzy,
not if "omnipresent" is our key word: then, the voice
of imprecation and measured shipwright details Noah heard,
the voice that gently blew on its waiting materials
to kindle a flame in the brain of Joan of Arc, would speak
with authority through the stately, circumjubilant rings
of Saturn; and no less so through the nipple rings
on sale this week only at the Dundjinn. Fraught. Consoling.
Oblique. Instructional. Through the bush
that revealed the journey's way to Moses, and still it was not
        consumed;
as well as through the rubbish fire I smote
out of existence just last night in the darkened parking lot

in back of Fat Cat's Snookers & Ale. We needn't be
penitential or mediumistic. Once I heard it
during a visit to my father's hospital bed, a voice
of staticky whisper and prophecy, from the catheter tube
like an alien parasite tentacle extruding
through the artificially widened pee-hole . . . I with bluster,
and he with courage, talking of anything *but*
that monstrous presence; and all the while, the voice
of the universe itself was sermonizing to me
about all of our futures. I don't know you, I don't know
how strong you are or not, and so I won't report the specifics.
Ever since, however, I've been aware of warning and directive
in the least of things—of utterance
apportioned through the units of the world. If there could be
a vocabulary in which "choral" and "totality" were
synonymous. The voice of the cure for, oh let's say
lymphoma, up in the clouds somewhere, the realm of dreams
somewhere; and also the voice of the eggy precipitate that's crusted
to the bottom of the beaker in a failed lab experiment.
The voice that booms through the coliseum gut of the whale;
the voice of a cricket's troubadour legs. Nor can we overlook
—if this is deity we're talking about—the voice
that's also manifest in anything inert.
The voice in a proton. In a polymer. We needn't be
repentant, or fundamentalist, or agog
with the spirit of serpent tongues and myrrh.
We needn't be messianic or scriptural. Once
I heard it in bed, in a woman's body: even silent,
even asleep in afterlove, each inch of her was delegated
to speak of unboundaried pleasure
on behalf of the voice. There is no seeming deaf to that
communication, and not to its calms, and not
to its indictments. And we needn't be washed in the blood of the lamb
or the ape or the triceratops. Proximity
is considerable: the plastic voice
in the dollar ninja action figure might be more persuasive
than the thunderation shaking forth in the stone voice
of Mount Rushmore, of those monumental Buddhas
that could serve as seven-level parking garages with room
in the skull left over to be an astronomical observatory.

We needn't be ressurectionist or apocalyptic or wicca-wise.
The voice in the cracking surface of seventeenth-century
Flemish painting. "Phlegmish," a student wrote: mistakenness
is also a proper vehicle for the voice. The voice
inside the smell in the rubber nose
the party clown first whiffs and then forgets,
after rubberbanding it to his face. The voice in a spirochete.
The stars are loud. The emptiness between the stars is loud.
Not that I've ever intended this to be a treatise
in defense of the existence of God; for all I know,
there isn't one, there's just an abstract notion
of a ventriloquist's puppet, fashioned
after ourselves, so that we can speak to ourselves
inarguably, and touch upon the mysteries.
I've heard it at moments of such intense sublimity
of thought and higher purpose, I felt bodiless;
I've heard it in simply resting my head
against my wife, at night, the reddish down upon her
here and there as eloquent as the twenty-first century fibers
of any access screen.
She may be a television, at that.
The light inside, and the coiled tubes.

Domestic Espionage

1.

On the inner side of the door: a couple in bed; out here,
a man is kneeled, squinting through the keyhole.
In a similar scene, a man is kneeling in front of a flap
of the world, and on its other side: another world,
the starry gears, the planets and the moons, that turn
the music of the universe. There's also the engraving
of a woman (could she even be a nun? an errant nun?
it's hard to see beneath the crumpled cloak-and-hood) who's crouched
conspicuously (at least to our gaze), her ear against
the side of a confessional booth. And so there's vast
iconographic lineage behind this scene I remember
—my sister and I are now supposed to be asleep, but
we've positioned ourselves as silent as dust
by the door at the top of the stairs, to strain to listen
for the magic (or terror) (or prestidigitorial power)
(or simple, blushing foolishness) on naked display when our parents
entertained the Kirschners and Appelbaums. In the standard
interpretation of this, we're little thieves: we want
to leave with a gleaming strand or two of conversation that's
not properly ours. And yet it was the opposite, too:
we longed to donate, to join it. We wanted whatever
small cork chips of childish majesty or depredation that bobbed
in us, to enter that swirl
—to enter the greater current.

2a.

"You goddam shit!" she hears herself saying, no,
screaming, releasing it less as spoken words and more
an explosion that might take out the windows and doors
as it flattens her fourteen-year-old son,
the goddam shit . . . she's said it, she
who forbids even something so mild as hell or damn
in the house, but *this* . . . she's known of course he might
be found out searching for some porn site on the Web,
she isn't naive, he *is* an adolescent boy, they *do* explore
this need inside them in an effort to define it, so
okay, some place called Tease-and A's or Hotchicks, that
would be ugly but that would still be understandable—but
this, this site on how to construct a *pipe bomb?* . . .
He just stands there, his entire body trembling,
not at being caught, he has no shame in this, there's just
the knowledge she's betrayed him, that she's gone
"behind his back" to check the trail of his browsings,
and a righteous anger is in him now like red
at hurricane force, "You bitch, you bitch," he says and in
the second of silence that follows, the moon is gouged
all over again from the ribs of the earth, and soil
thunders up in a column that when it falls will fill
the seas like a cold paste, and the continents split apart,
and the entire species dies out.

2b.

In the gardens off the nursing home this afternoon,
the sun could calm a caffeine freak to drowsiness.
The flowers are attended by bees as round as tugboats.
Sheets of a sleepy perfume are covering everything.
I'm lingering here while my friend M. is inside
with her eighty-year-old mother. I could almost think
these gardens generate a secret herbal wonder that prohibits aging,
everything is so still . . . then . . . "O *Jesus* LOOK!
Will you LOOK at this!"—and when I hustle into the hallway,
    "Albert,
LOOK"—in her opened palm are ten gel capsules, scarlet-red, that
    puddle there
as if she's revealing stigmata. "I was searching in her dresser
    drawer . . ."
she's breathless from only that little speech, she's rapidly matching
the vibrant red in her hand, like some example
of protective coloration at work, ". . . and LOOK!" By now a forming
    crowd
is at the door. "She SAVED these UP, she was going to KILL herself
—WEREN'T YOU!" So this is love, mutated
under pressure into something unrecognizable as love.
"O Jesus GOD! You . . . bitch!" And as she says it
—she tells me this later—her son, who's dead for five years now,
is in the room, is staring at her with that same accusatory word
corrupting the air between them. "I'm WARNING you . . . if you kill
    yourself . . ."
each syllable receives the measured emphasis of her finger
dabbing its permanence into the fabric of this sad unraveling day
". . . I SWEAR to GOD I'm going to hurt you."

Lucia Perillo

First Epistle of Lucia to Her Old Boyfriends

Not infrequently I find myself wondering which of you are dead
now that it's been so long since I have had a boyfriend
for whom this wonder would be a somewhat milder version of
the way our actual parting went—i.e., with me not wondering
but outright wishing that an outright lightning bolt
would sail sharply into your thick heads.

Can I plead youth now over malign intent?
And does my moral fiber matter anyhow
since I have not gone forth and et cetera'd—
i.e., don't my absent children's nondepletion of the ozone layer
give me some atmospheric exchange credits under the Kyoto Treaty
to release the fluorocarbons of these unkind thoughts?

Anyhow what is the likelihood of you old boyfriends reading this
even if you are not dead? Be assured your end is hypothetical.
Also be assured I blush most furiously
whenever that tower room in Ensenada comes to mind
where the mescal functioned as an exchange credit for those lies you told
about your Alford pleas and your ex-wives who turned out not ex at all.

Anyhow the acid rain has caused my lightning to go limp
over bungalows where you have partial custody of your teenagers,
AA affirmations magnet-ed to the fridge
from which your near-beers sweat as you wonder if I'm dead,
since the exchange for this-here wonder is your wonder about me.
Even though it shows my nerve—to think you'd think of me at all—

I await word of your undeadness

P.S. along with your mild version of my just reward.

"Pig Meat Is What I Crave"

Every time I see this white bluesman on TV, I wonder:
will he ever take off his Zorro hat
or that black shirt with the iron cross

hanging in its open neck?
Between his hat and his soul patch, his pinkie ring and neckerchief,
his silver-tipped speckled snakeskin cockroach kickers:

will he always show up dressed like this,
won't he ever change?
Space-time says no—because he is dead,

however late into the night he dawdles.
And I have channel-surfed over him so many times
I could map a star chart of his beard-follicles.

But the blues is a form
in which the little that gets said gets repeated
if just to occupy space, the space, the space

where trouble would otherwise set down its landing gear.
The fight starts when we stop dancing,
our heads will pound when we stop drinking,

the baby's cry follows the come-cry's silence,
and when we fall asleep—
that's when the car goes off the road.

So let me push back fate by these four seconds
with a roll call of some simple graves:
Blind Lemon Jefferson, Blind Boy Fuller, Blind Willie Johnson or
     McTell.

And while I paused to list them
who knows what corner I didn't go round in a hurry
to collide with the fang of my worst luck?

In this hour of infomercials
when the moon is full
and the white ghost sings

twelve bars, like the bars of a Havahart trap
baited with sludge like peanut butter or honey,
a substance as sticky as the song's complaint.

His groans make my heart slink off like a possum,
not the sharpest tool in Darwin's kit bag—
just the beast with the whopping-most fifty teeth

and that terrifying-most tail
glimpsed at night in the alley,
retracting like an electric cord into the weeds.

Stephen Dobyns

Getting Used To It

He walks his arc from dark to dark
and now the time has come to consider
his maturity, what others might call
his old age, even his declining years.

It rests beside him on a park bench
and others might think it's a gorilla suit
with wooden teeth and the fur falling out
in clumps. But of course he knows better.

This is wisdom in disguise, he thinks,
this is my accumulated credibility.
Nice gorilla suit, people call out as they
dash toward the park's many pleasures.

Maturity comes in a billion shapes
and his looks like a great ape. It's not
sexy, he thinks, it won't keep me warm
at night. But being a good sport, he wrestles it

over his head and chest, wiggles his hips,
pulls up the feet. It's an older model
and tight around the middle. Whatever
the case, it's soon locked in place. I can

get used to this, he thinks, it's only a rental:
a costume I've accepted on a bet,
a temporary aggravation. He wants
to explain this to the passersby, but

in their rush to seize the most from life,
all are dying to escape. As they sprint toward
the park's promised pleasures, he notices
an indistinct shape slithering across the grass

behind each: a riffle of wind or bit of litter,
maybe a snake or frisky rat. It's only
a shadow, they insist. But didn't he read
as a little boy one summer long ago,

at the barber shop in a magazine called True
or Real Tales that carved into the stone gates
to the Unknown it said: Today's Shadow
Is Tomorrow's Gorilla Suit Getting Ready?

Nap Time

"Knock, knock," the Avenging Angel shouts.
The sinner sighs and asks, "Knock, knock who?"
"Abyss." "Abyss who?" "Abyss 'eeing you

in hell!" The sinner rolls his eyes. "Knock, knock,"
        the angel repeats, and so he keeps it up
        all week, until the sinner begs for mercy.

This is a kinder, gentler avenging angel,
        driving his clients nuts with knock-knock jokes
        ever since God has chosen to lower the bar

to heaven, opening the door to pagans,
Buddhists, Muslims, Hindus, Jews and even
the occasional Satanist. Still, the blue

and everlasting expanse of infinitude
has been growing progressively bare
        as more and more of the immortal dead

are opting to sit eternity out. "Maybe
next time," shrugs a potential saint,
        "I'd rather try the never-ending dark."

One claims the need to rest, another states
        he has no wish to play the harp, a third
        gripes about the interminable small talk,

and so they leave the Pearly Gates to enter
        silence. Can any good idea continue
        as a good idea forever? I guess not.

Tony Hoagland

Plastic

One could probably explain the whole world in terms of the plastic
used now for almost everything—the little ivory forks at picnics
                and green toy dinosaurs in playrooms everywhere;

the rooks and pawns of cheap 4.95 chess sets made in the People's
                         Republic of China

and those Tupperware containers which open with a perfect quiet pop
to yield the tuna fish sandwich
about to enter the mouth of the secretary on his lunchbreak.

You could talk about how the big molecules were bound in chains
by chemical reactions, then liquefied and poured like soup

into intricate factory molds
for toy soldiers and backscratchers, airsick bags and high-tech Teflon
   roofracks;

you could mull over the ethics of enslaving matter
                even while feeling admiration for the genius it takes

to persuade a molecule to become part of a casserole container.

And what about plastic that has become dear to you?
Personal plastic?
              —the toothbrush and the flip-flops,

the hollow plastic Easter egg which held jellybeans inside,
the twelve-inch vinyl disk that in l976 brought you Jezebel Brown and
             the Attorneys of Cool?

plastic companions into which the lonely heart was poured,
                    which gave it color and a shape?

—Or in another case, the blue polyethylene water bottle
I saw sitting on a table in the park on Saturday

between two people having a conversation about their relationship,

which you could tell was probably near its end
since the various lubrications
                    usually coating the human voice

were all worn away, leaving just the rough, gritty surfaces
of need and fear
                    exposed and rubbing on each other.

I wonder if it would have done any good
if I had walked over and explained a few things to them

about plastic?
about how it is so much easier to stretch than
                              human nature,

which accounts for some of the strain imposed on
                    the late 20th century self,
occasionally causing what has been called Interpersonal Adhesive
    Malfunction.

They might have been relieved to know that science had a name

for their feelings at that precise moment of modern living,

which may be why each of them kept reaching out
to seize the plastic water bottle and suck from it
                              in fierce little hydraulic gulps

as if the water was helping them to wash down
                              something hard to ingest;
    or the bottle was a lifevest keeping them afloat on open sea—

though their pink elastic lips, wrapped around the stem of the bottle
were so much more beautiful than plastic

and the smooth ripple
of their flexible muscular throats
made the only sound audible

above the tough, indifferent silence
                              now starting to stretch over everything.

Disaster Movie

You were a jumbo jet, America,
        gone down in the jungle in my dream.

It must have been Borneo, or someplace tropical like that,
because vines had strangled the propellers into stillness,
rust was already licking the battered silver wings.

Monkeys had commandeered the cockpit
and were getting drunk
        on the miniature bottles of vodka and Jack Daniels,

wearing the orange safety vests backwards
and spinning in the empty swivel chairs.

In the first class cabin, the first class passengers
had finished the last of the Chicken Kiev
        and were barricaded in,

while outside the economy fliers had gathered by the defunct fuselage
to take a vote
on whether to wait for rescue or to try to rescue themselves.

I couldn't believe that my twisted subconscious
would crashtest a whole nation to make a point;
that my disgust with cell phones and beauty pageants would drive me

to ram it headfirst into the side of a hill,—its wings snapped off,
its captain decapitated,

its dependence on foreign oil
brought to a sudden conclusion.

And sure, I knew that this apocalypse was a thin disguise
for my pitiful fear of being no good at ordinary life.

But what was sweet in the dream was the quiet
courage of those little people:

someone using duct tape to make a bed out of flotation cushions;
the stewardess limping past on crutches as night seeped in.

The huge cracked tube of the plane
laid out in pieces like a shiny broken toy.

An AA meeting in progress by one of the enormous, flattened tires.
And a woman singing in the dusk

as she tended a fire
made of safety manuals and self-help books.

Rhythm and Blues

And five months later
the snow on the far side of the street had melted,
                    the season changing again and

I was still thinking of my friend Rolf Jordahl
and how strange it was to be sitting in his backyard
                            after his funeral last year

watching the vines stir softly on the trellis
while his sister and her friends got drunk
                    in clusters on the patio—

I saw the empty dogfood bowl
                someone had taken the trouble to wash out,
                        the red plastic O like an open mouth,

and in the bedroom, the shirts piled up on his bed
                        for people to go through—

I tell you, it was pretty unpleasant
to watch all of his possessions
                    giving up his fingerprints like that—

as someone put on one of his records
        and Etta James began to sing *I Hate To*
                    See That Evening Sun Go Down,

inside her voice the little bloody sun
            going down in the kitchen window of each syllable,

as I thought to myself Yes, this is what it comes to—
        always a sad woman standing at a sink
                    scraping the old food from the plates—

But it will never be alright with me, this moving on,
            the way people let themselves
                        get away with it,

as if life was a series of hotel rooms
                              we leave behind
for someone else to clean,

and memory a little glass of wine
you sip for pleasure and then put down.

I watched the people at that party
                    like a policeman taking notes,
sorting out the real tears from the sentimental ones,

noticing the exact moment when
grief smeared into self-pity
                    and the ones with unhappy marriages
                                        started looking around—

I guess judgment was my way of remembering my friend,
I guess I thought I was defending him
                              from being forgotten,

holding on with one hand and
godamming everybody else
                    for not holding on tighter,

but I finally couldn't sort it out

and even my self-righteousness began to wane and lose its torchlike
    force,

as the sky above the yard grew dim,
                    and people moved indoors.

By that time I had one of Rolf's shirts under my arm,
                    and was talking to the sister from Minneapolis,

noticing how brave her nipples were, upright
even in that hour of grief,

as she raised her glass and said,
Did you ever consider that maybe
                              Time is sipping us?

rolling us around inside its mouth like Pinot Noir,

smacking its lips, considering our vintage
before it spits us out again
                        into the life that we have left?

Then she took her coat and disappeared
                        and I was standing on the edge of a crowd,

looking at a roomful of faces
                        flushed with the effort of forgetting.

This has been the year I will remember
                        as the one in which I wore Rolf's shirt,

like a secret and a pledge;
like a penance and critique;
like a fashion statement and an antique.

Each time I put it on I felt my arm push through
one of the holes he left,

and sometimes, I was surprised not to find him there ahead of me;
and sometimes I just forgot whose shirt it was,

—taking the sleeve between my forefinger and thumb,
and rubbing it absent-mindedly,

or sometimes slipping my hand between the buttons
to touch myself.

Jazz

For Barry Rackner

I was driving home that afternoon
in some dilated condition of sensitivity
of the kind known only to certain heroic poets
and more or less almost everybody else:

the sun of six PM glaring orangely through the trees
as through the bars of some kind of cage
and the poor citizens of Pecore Street waiting for the bus
with their sorrowful posture and bad feet-

I admit when I'm in one of these moods I find it
a little too easy to believe the trees are suffering;
to see the twisted branches as outstretched arthritic hands,
and the Spanish moss dripping from their scabby limbs
as parasitic bunting.

Someone had given me a jazz CD
he had thought I would enjoy,
but the song unfurling on the stereo that day,
it seemed a kind of torture-music,

played by wildly unhappy musicians
on instruments that had been bent in shipping,
then harnessed by some masochist composer
for an experiment on the nature of obstruction.

But of all the shrieking horns and drums
it was the passionate effort of a certain defective trumpet
to escape from its predetermined plot
that seemed to be telling a story that I knew:

veering back and forth, banging off of walls,
dripping a trail of blood
until finally it shattered through a window and disappeared.

For some reason I didn't understand,
it had to suffer before it was allowed to rest.
It was permitted to rest before being recaptured.

That was part of the composition.
That was the only kind of freedom
we were ever going to know.

Mark Halliday

Dreamhooked

In a blue notebook in maybe 1983
I drafted an Ode to Sexual Fantasy
which probably was quite bad because too simple and obvious
and much less merry and incisive than I imagined;
well, I must have known it wasn't great
since I let it stay in the notebook
and left the notebook in a drawer in my father's house in Vermont—

I don't think I wanted him to see it
but I guess he probably did on some dull Saturday
when he was trying to clear old files and drawers and shelves—

I feel queasy thinking of him reading my Ode to Sexual Fantasy—
him in his seventies, me in my thirties—
my father standing there in the dusty quiet house
reading my lines about how sexual fantasy helps keep us alive—
stirring the embers—sustaining the dream-hope for Shangri-La;

Surely I had two or three metaphors not utterly flaccid?—
And I hope the poem included also an awareness
that sexual fantasy may also be part of what ages and kills us,
because always there arrives the moment of realizing
how idiotically repetitious the fantasies are—
bosoms bottom boom bosoms bottom boom whum yum—
and how pathetically distant from what will happen
for the dreamhooked boy of thirty-eight or seventy-three . . .

I do hope that's all there in the Ode
because it would imply I wasn't just being sheerly stupidly ordinary

when I wrote it—so my father reading it
alone in the dusty Vermont house
would see that his son was not just stupidly ordinary—

But then also he would feel sad, sad to be at the mercy of the images—
Jane Russell, Marilyn Monroe, Raquel Welch,
a certain secretary in 1974,
the fabulous warm unreachable weighty passionating shapes—
sad to be reminded that he still had not escaped;
and sad to see how garishly and helplessly his son had inherited the
    dreamhook;

So I'm afraid my failed poem may have added one more shade
to the layered sadness of being seventy-three or seventy-eight
one long Saturday alone in Vermont in a jumbled house.

He kept himself alive, though,
not without some gladness till he was eighty-nine,
nourished as well as ravaged by irresistible wishing.

And if at the age of fifty-six I find that blue notebook
in an old file or box there will be
the shadow of a tremor of embarrassment
and a distant low pulsing of sadness
as if a low note were softly played
several times on a piano downstairs;

nourished but also ravaged we are
by irresistible failures of representing
—representing because
the actual breathing talking perceptive woman is *much* too
    complicated;

And I'll keep the notebook in a pile of old things
that represent me—the acorn, Daddy, not too far from the tree—

And just for a minute, that night,
a ghost of Maggie or Liz or Patty or Tracy will visit me, radiant—

Muck-Clump

My wife was being too *busy* around the kitchen one morning
I think to give herself the sense of being on top of things
and when I poured a bowl of Shredded Wheat Spoonfuls for Devon
my wife bustled over and said "Oh Devon likes to have more cereal
    than that"
so she poured more Spoonfuls on top of the considerable number I had
    poured.
This griped me because now it was as if I hadn't given Devon her
    breakfast
because it might as well have been my wife who did it all
which would imply that I wasn't really making a contribution,
as if I were just a log of driftwood on the sand of time
while everyone else built the boats and caught the fish
and made the whole human drama fare forward against the void.

So I watched Devon pour a lot of milk on her Shredded Spoonfuls
and I figured she would hardly eat half of them
and when she went out to the school bus there would be
this awful soggy mass of decomposing cereal left behind
which would resemble the way I sometimes see myself
so I figured then I could show the bowl to my wife
and I'd say "Do you think Devon got enough cereal?"
and the moment of sarcasm would be exquisite.
While Devon ate Spoonfuls I tied her shoes—I did accomplish that—
and I imagined how I would say it with measured irony
that would sting slightly but also come across as witty—
"Do you think Devon got enough cereal?"—I would say it
and then vigorously dump the sodden milky muck-clump into the
    trash.
It would be a moment in which I would be quite noticeably
on top of things . . . Then the bus came
and Devon hoisted her backpack and hurried outside, calling
    Goodbye,

and I saw with astonishment that her cereal bowl was empty.
How was I going to deal with this? It wouldn't be fair
to be angry at Devon for her unreasonable appetite; but
I could possibly complain about my wife's failure to provide
a more balanced breakfast for our daughter—but I sensed
that this challenge would backfire because my wife is the one
who really does think about nutrition and besides there were, actually,
some strawberries on Devon's placemat.
So I decided to rise above the entire episode, to be large-minded,
to wash a few dishes nonchalantly and read the newspaper
and make an insightful remark about something in the news.
Awareness of a larger world, after all, is
a central part of being mature, which is
something I want to believe I am—
when you see some old chunk of driftwood on the beach
you might say "That looks so calm, so peaceful"
or you might say "That is so dry and dead"
but you don't say "That is really mature."

Susan Wood

Horoscope

It's almost my birthday, but not quite, thank God, because
who'd want a horoscope like this on her birthday?

Take precautions today. Evil may come your way.
Because evil is such an over-the-top word, such

a nightmare-on-elm-street word. I mean, it could've said,
"Trouble may come your way," but evil? Not that

I don't believe in it, of course. Who wouldn't these days?
Decades of it, centuries. Hitler, Pol Pot, Idi Amin,

the usual suspects, not to mention countless other lackeys
and minor functionaries, the father who scalded the baby,

put out his cigarettes on her tender backside, the loser boyfriend
who shot the aspiring actress right in front of her mother

on a sidewalk in Chinatown. Or the serial killer everyone describes
as "polite" and "charming," whose face is all over the TV today,

the one who haunted south Louisiana through which I have so often
traveled alone, driving over the spooky swamp between Lafayette

and Baton Rouge, where there is no way off the interstate for miles
except the exit at Whiskey Bay, where one of the bodies

was found, haunted even Breaux Bridge, where the Sunday
after Christmas I ate crawfish etoufée at Mulate's Cajun Restaurant,

the band playing at one o'clock in the afternoon and couples
in matching outfits dancing the day away. Oh, I could go on

and on. Some days the grease of grief covers everything,
a thin film like the one that covers the body in the river. Yesterday

my friend, the most beautiful woman I know, was speaking
of sadness, and just for a moment I thought if I were

that beautiful I'd never be sad about anything, but then
I felt ashamed because I know sadness

is an equal-opportunity emotion and despair
can lead you around by the nose no matter who you are.

Remember when we were so avid for life we beat like little moths
around the days as though they were shining lamps?

Now, some days, I think merely to get up,
to make coffee and take the dog out into the May morning, to put

your face up close to the pink face of the odorless, frustrating
hibiscus is an act of endless courage. But last night

at a party I held a baby for an hour and he curled into me
like a new leaf, and today there is a family of cardinals

in the Japanese maple and nearby a mockingbird barking and cackling
and dive-bombing the gray cat who would eat the baby birds if he
    could.

And he could. And still the mockingbird will go on singing
in the privet hedge the whole May night. I can think of that couple

at Mulate's, their white shirts embroidered all over with red
    poinsettias.
Imagine her bending over her needle night after night and the tender
    way

he puts his palm on her back when they dance. And I have the
    memory
of my handsome young man of a son striding toward me

across Union Station, Baltimore, and his face when he sees me
and sweeps me up, apparently having forgotten all the reasons he had
    not to

speak to me last year. Nearby a covey of teenage girls keeps looking
his way, a little like newly hatched birds themselves, all legs and eyes,

despite their bare midriffs and low-rider cutoffs. Caleb just laughs.
"When I have daughters," he says, taking my arm, "they'll wear

baggy jeans and big T-shirts that say *I love my daddy*, and they'll always
love me best." They won't, of course, but for now

I can dream these girls are his girls and they have come with him
to the train station to meet me, who has traveled far into the future

just to see them, these girls who beat around us
like those moths around lamps, their wings little sparks of flame.

I Got a Mind to Ramble

Alberta Hunter at the Cookery, 1981

Winter, deep dark, the Village streets deserted, so cold even the
    homeless
have disappeared, and my friend and I are walking to the Cookery,
University Place and Eighth Street, both of us recently divorced
and so much alike—literary, smart, neurotic, a little narcissistic—

that her ex-husband keeps asking me out, but I don't want to trade
my old unhappy life for its identical twin. The air icy with our talk,
those nights examining our marriages over and over, like Darwin
examining his earthworms, except the men are always the worms

and we're the survival of the fittest, first ones off
the sinking ship of marriage. It'll take years
to admit our own worminess. Oh, we're shameless,
wearing our heavy coats of sadness, our guilt-tight gloves

like decorations. All we want is transformation—
I got a mind to ramble, but I don't know where to go—
the Tropics, bikinis and Ban de Soleil, pina coladas
at the swim-up bar, and long-lashed pool boys leering

from the cabanas. I'm in love with someone else, someone
who isn't in love with me, and I don't want to be.
At 14 Susan Sontag had a crush on Thomas Mann
while I had a crush on Ray Weems, the quarterback, so what hope

is there for me at 34 in love with the grownup equivalent
of a football hero? At least we have the good grace to be sick
of ourselves, a little bit anyway. Inside the Cookery, the air's
heavy with smoke, steam heat, the crowd hushed

and expectant, and then the spotlight comes up and there she is,
a tiny woman filling the room, bangle earrings almost big as her head,
—poor Memphis black child, Chicago potato-peeler, star, then nurse,
then star again, the latest sensation at 85. To sing the blues

is not to have the blues, which are, after all, less about sadness
than triumph and revenge, and she doesn't,
this high-yellow gal with the Indian nose, though she knows
we think she's a cutie pie, Miss Thing, and she's playing us,

jiving, the way she teases "I Got a Mind to Ramble," slapping
her hip like a tambourine, the dark, rich voice now a wink, now
a growl, a voice someone called "a contralto that wears boots."
"Ladies," she says, dispensing advice between songs,

"if you tell a man you love him, you're in a bad fix.
He's gonna ruin you. Don't let that happen to you, honey."
And then she segues into "Down Hearted Blues," a song
she wrote in 1922, fingers snapping, eyes rolling—

Gee! but it's hard to love someone
When that someone don't love you,
I'm so disgusted, heartbroken too,
I've got the down hearted blues . . .

Got the world in a jug, got the stopper in my hand,
Got the world in a jug, got the stopper in my hand,
And if you want me, you must come under my command—

And aren't we transformed for a moment?
For an evening we believe her, or believe we do,
women who don't need men, who don't need love, the world
and everything in it for once at our command.

What did we know? Not much. Surely not how long it takes,
the slow, blind ramble toward change, to arrive, if ever, at something
provisional as wisdom. I wonder now if she saw, when she looked out
into that dark night of white faces, how lost we were on the starless
    road,

how alone and thirsty, no jug, no stopper anywhere in sight.
And maybe she might even have pitied us a little, this old woman
who'd spent one of her lifetimes mastering a kind of Braille,
emptying the bed pans of the dying, thumbing shut the dumb eyes of
    the dead.

Jon Schneider

What Do I Recommend?

It's not on the menu, but we've got a waffle iron,
      and when it's hot, boy,
   you can smell it a bike ride away,

and the sinners come running with forked tongues
      and knives in their back pockets,
   because, Baby, it's like you're cheating

on somebody when I set down that inch-thick
      dimpled sugar cookie,
   peanut-buttered over, with a Chiquita

dance floor and thin slices of sweet peaches,
      crunched pecans and shredded
   coconut climbing up a Cool Whip mountain,

all liquored up and laced with wavy lines of chocolate
      sauce and honey dripping
   off the edges of your plate, and you can spank

yourself later or fudge some numbers
      on your calorie chart
   because this is that sweet girl who never says no,

sugar-lipped and messy with Hershey colored hair,
      this is what you count
   your quarters for, and listen, I've had my hand

stabbed twice for trying to take an empty plate,
      so I won't even touch it
   until you leave because it's something people eat

slow on purpose, bite after bite, biting their lips,
      and swirling the underside
   of sticky forks across gooey plates

with tiny crumbs of just about everything leftover,
      and if a woman were a waffle
   or a waffle were a woman this is how I'd order mine.

Josh Bell

Vince Neil Meets Josh in a Chinese Restaurant in Malibu (after Ezra Pound)

Back when my voicebox
was a cabinet-full of golden vibrators, and my hair
fell white across the middle of my back
like a child's wedding dress,
I made love to at least a dozen girls
dressed up to look like me: the hotel bed a sky
filled with the spastic flock
of our South-Flying mic scarves,
the back of my head and the front
appearing simultaneously
in hotel mirrors, and the twin crusts of our make-up
sliding off into satin seas
like bits of California coast. I heard my own lyrics
coming out of the greasy tent
of their beautiful wigs, my lyrics driven back
towards me, poled into me, demanding of me
the willing completion of vague circus acts
I'd scribbled down, once, on the back of a golf card
or a piece of toilet paper. Sometimes I myself
wonder what I was thinking then, but those words
went on to live forever, didn't they, radioed out
into the giant Midwestern backseat
and blasted into kneecaps and tailbones
by that endless tongue of berber carpeting
blanketing the American suburbs, boys and girls
strung like paper lanterns from here to Syracuse
along my microphone cord. Who rocks you now

rocks you always, I told them all,
and all of them somehow wearing
a homemade version of the same leather pants
I'd chosen to wear on stage that night;
all of them hoping to enter me—to enter anyone—
the way they thought I entered them,
and the way I entered them was wishing
I was somewhere else, or wishing I was
the someone else who'd come along
to enter me, which was the same thing.
I am no fag, my new friend.
Love in battle conditions requires a broad
taxonomy, queerness has its ever-more-visible degrees.
Josh, I know you know what I'm talking about,
you have the build of a stevedore. Which reminds me—more shrimp
fried rice?—as a child in Nanjing,
I sculled the junks for my bread and I slept
in a hovel along the Chiang Jiang River.
In a cage there, I bred mice who built their nests
from the frayed rope I'd taken from the decks, and one Spring,
when the babies did not emerge, I lifted
up the rock that hid them, and I found
they'd grown together, fused with each other
and the tendrils of the nest. I held them up, eleven blind tomatoes
wriggling on a blackened vine. My friends and I
performed many surgeries. And now you come to me
in this Chinese restaurant in Malibu,
asking if you can help me. Please tell *Circus Magazine* I love them
forever, and please pass Pamela this message:
If you get back to Malibu by springtime, drop by the boathouse,
and I'll rock your ass as far as Cho-Fu-Sa.

We Will Begin By Placing You In This Bag

There's friend A, the totally sexy one.
And there's friend C, he made the sculpture of the ice cube for A, the
  totally sexy one.
We don't know where B has gotten to, B who is married to C, B
  probably out breaking
      windows, writing a poem about how beauty is the knife.
D is not our friend, D the towheaded one, she knows us through B, but
  we are being nice
      to D for now so maybe we can kiss her, D or B the poetess,
        whichever, so you can
          help us keep our cover
at least until E shows up, with her unfinished spy novel and her can of
  olives
for G and us. G and us we like to sleep when it's raining
and eat olives, to hell with girls, and you be G for awhile, we like you
  a lot, G, whoever
      you are, so unlike F, forget about F, with his silly complaints
        and his too-finished
          movie script, beginning with the phrase, "we open on
            the void," that F,
              strange F, we're starting to like F a little better
                now, yes F
                  is really starting to grow on us,
but we're telling you flat out we're in love with H, she wants to lick
  A's slender calves,
      we always love such lesbians as are unavailable to us, and H is
        also thinking
          about changing her name
to I, but we already have a friend named I, which I hates because it's
a girl's name, and I have come for the body of J
says K to J in the hallway. I have come for the body of K
booms M to K, looming up behind her, and L, who is standing behind
  him, slaps him
      on the back of the head, she is so jealous

of K, but not as jealous as N is of A, the totally sexy one, N who is our
girlfriend, our
girlfriend who went to prison with O, O of whom *we're*
jealous, who writes us
letters from prison assuring us we *should* be jealous,
saying sometimes
through the bars and in the prison yard the dew on
the grass
looks like little diamonds
she can't steal. Did anyone see where J went? J knows us through P
and P is standing
over there, trying to appear as if he is not wearing ladies
underpants, you'll
get so you can draw that expression from memory, but
wait, that's not P
after all, we don't know who that is, P went
home to New Hampshire and
anyway Q was not invited, what's she doing here?
Right there, standing at the punch bowl next to, wait a minute,
is that R?
We think it is. R, how are you, you can barely see the scar, and S so
handsome tonight
it makes T think of parakeets flying through
a scarf of rain, and U gets down on his knees before us all
which makes V think he's going to say a prayer or make a pass at A,
the totally sexy one, but it's
really that he's lost a contact lens, but which first thoughts V
confides to W, and that funny V, thinks W, always getting ecumenical,
but is *ecumenical*
the right word? thinks X, reading everyone's thoughts, that is so like X,
and then X says, as if it's
just hit her: "is it me, or did someone actually say *scarf of
rain?*"
and Y never shows up until late, and when she does come strolling
through the door
she is exactly sixteen minutes pregnant
and Z, whose house this is, who is our gracious host, you can bet he
makes a note of it.

What It's Like Outside

The great detective steps over the corpse and walks across the apartment to the open window, through which the killer's bullets entered the room. Using his pencil as a pointer, he sticks his hand out of the window, toward the building across the street, plotting the likely trajectory of the bullets. *There*, he says to the young lieutenant, and *There*. He puts his other hand out of the window, just to make sure, and then he pokes his head out, too. Though the forecast said rain, it's a beautiful day, and he stays that way a long time: half in, half out, eyes looking skyward, his pencil upraised like a baton. Soon, on the sidewalk below him, an orchestra begins to form. It seems there will be music after all! The violins appear, carrying folding chairs and music stands which they arrange according to the great detective's instructions. The cellos shout a greeting to the bassoons, who've just stepped off the downtown bus, and the young lieutenant produces a silver triangle from his pocket. When the lone oboist tests his reed—squink!—one by one the other instruments begin, and this is the great detective's favorite part: the sound of his orchestra warming up, an oblong planet, drifting through space along its weird english. But has anyone seen the first violin? She's never late, she's so talented. Oh there she is! There, crossing the street toward the orchestra, sandals slapping the pavement, her orange rain slicker popping with each step. The great detective smiles as she opens up her battered, black violin case. She's like a daughter to him, and in a moment he'll tap the window sill with his baton, and finally we in the audience can relax, because we know it's unlikely that anyone was murdered here, what with the first violin accounted for, and it being concert day.

Gerald Stern

Thom McCann

This was to be free of the burden of representation,
to put your feet in an x-ray machine and thereby
not only get cancer and not only get fitted up
with the perfect pair of shoes, but thence to grieve
how thin your bones looked, how like more like a bird
you were than an ape and how you grieved how huge
your feet were and you went to the machine oh every
ten minutes or so and how that leather pinched
for it was more cardboard than cow and how it was
inevitable the limping, it was called
the breaking in, I wanted to tell you this.

Blue Like That

She was a darling with her roses, though what I
like is lavender for I can dry it and
nothing is blue like that, so here I am,
in my arms a bouquet of tragic lavender,
the whole history of Southern France against my
chest, the fields stretching out, the armies
killing each other, horses falling, Frenchmen
dying by the thousands, though none for love.

Catherine Bowman

Sylvia Plath's Paper Dolls:
Gold Hostess Frock with Top Hat

Top hat, double-D breasts, a long-sleeved lion tamer's waistcoat, leather choker. A leather apron drafted from fairy-tale leftovers. A golden petticoat extracted from sunburst. She'll wear this tonight at the pleasantest of all social occasions, the little dinner. The beasting will begin at half past eight. Strawberries should be impaled on a fork. Tangerines, stripped of their skins, segmented and eaten with the fingers. A handled cup is held with the thumb just above the support grip; the little finger follows the curve. Lift her apron up and it's all lion radiance. After supper, a parlor game, the adults-only lion roar.

Sylvia Plath's Paper Dolls: Three Black Skirts

Three black skirts. Three black rooks. Three black tulips. The pupils widen and widen until all is raw ink. Now it is nighttime—zero brilliance—the dark half-world, the lower world, the other hemisphere. Three black glass blown lamps for the casino. Place your bets for the blackjack's ace. Three black skirts in eight black shades: grotto lung, torch god, urge, uh, French noon, egg foo, yuletide, and her brother's masculine typewriter. Mathematical skirts. They are clocks. Little obsidian mountains, tick-tock, there's no one on top. Three black skirts! Full and tight as a train whistle. Dilation distilled, only train tunnels here. Black dove annunciation. Three glass black bells. Good luck comes in threes. Three times the black dog swims in a circle. Conversational volcano jars. Three black skirts! Flared heaviness just right for a belt. Lady of the house, she must invent only black flowers, tend her black hens and their precious black eggs. She keeps the floors polished and the hearts fattened in the state room. *The sea spilling through pell-mell blue-black.* Pick a skirt, any skirt: number one, number two, or number three. And in the evening him—pink paws—a lick of milk along a royal highway. Now, let's paint mouths.

Sylvia Plath's Paper Dolls:
Midnight Blue Gown with Cape

Gown sculpted from night sky, stitched with Eve's tears. Stars spin around the skin-tight blue tent. She is ready for anything blue now. Midnight blue cape. Midnight ocean. A bodice-wrapped full-moon reflection, moonskin across a low tide. A gown lined with two magenta waves: wave and inner wave solidified for a viola lesson or an evening of rabbiting. Hunting fish-glass in a gown of cave-glow. Curvy, up against blue French doors. French doors always just barely ajar. She strokes a slutty blue kitten, gazes out at a man in black on the magenta breakwater. *Venus, anti-Venus, Venus, anti-Venus* she counts on the petals of an upside-down flower. Curvy blue, she plucks a pair of children's scissors hanging from a tree and cuts five yellow stars out of the sky. She places one star on her hip, one between her breasts, one on each slipper, and one on her matching midnight blue mask. The great Connemara sky cows' butter, the sugar-and-butter stars.

Billy Collins

The Man Who Could Read a Book through a Wall

> "[Andrew Jackson] Davis could accomplish apparently
> miraculous things such as reading books through walls . . ."
>
> David S. Reynolds, *Walt Whitman's America*

There is no telling why Whitman found him
intriguing enough to follow,
this Andrew Jackson Davis, the Seer of Poughkeepsie.

Was it the possibility that such things were possible,
or was it the sheer audacity of the claim
and the spectacle of a man who would stand in a room

and recite a long, memorized passage
of *The Old Curiosity Shop* or *Emma*
while a copy of that book lay open on a table in the next room

Someone—and who better than Whitman—
might have told Andrew Jackson Davis
that it was remarkable enough to look *at* a wall,

to follow the maze of a wallpaper's pattern,
a repetition of fleurs de lis,
a configuration of vines and peonies,

to walk closer and examine the oil painting
hanging there in a wooden frame,
the one of a sailing ship foundering in a storm at sea,

to wonder about the painter, now long dead,
then to notice for the first time
three tiny men clinging to the rigging.

I want to imagine Whitman taking Andrew Jackson Davis
by the coat sleeve over to a window
and showing him the crows on the lawn,

the shade trees of the cemetery beyond.
And if the two of them had gone out walking
in the streets of Manhattan

then along the grassy banks of the Harlem River,
perhaps that evening Andrew Jackson Davis
would have read a book sitting alone in a chair at home,

his wife sewing on a button in the next room,
content within the four walls of a room,
returned at last to his remarkable normality.

Adage

When it's late at night and branches
are banging against the windows,
you might think that love is just a matter

of leaping out of the frying pan of yourself
into the fire of someone else,
but it's a little more complicated than that.

It's more like trading the two birds
who might be hiding in that bush
for the one you are not holding in your hand.

A wise man once said that love
was like forcing a horse to drink
but then everyone stopped thinking of him as wise.

Let us be clear about something.
Love is not as simple as getting up
on the wrong side of the bed wearing the emperor's clothes.

No, it's more like the way the pen
feels after it has defeated the sword.
It's a little like the penny saved or the nine dropped stitches.

You look at me through the halo of the last candle
and tell me love is an ill wind
that has no turning, a road that blows no good,

but I am here to remind you,
as our shadows tremble on the walls,
that love is the early bird who is better late than never.

Waiting

What better time to step up to the plate
of philosophy than when waiting
for a bus, a phone call, or for someone to arrive at a bar
where you have been sitting for a good hour?

Is this the natural progress of life,
I wondered as I ordered a second drink—
just millions of moments flashing by
and disappearing into a vast building of brick?

I pictured it standing by the side of a river
where a man in a hat is walking along,
where a child leans on an iron railing
as the boats pass each other on the flowing water.

And then I actually recognized it
as none other than the Battersea Power Station
considered by some to be the most
stunning edifice in all of greater London.

But who would believe that the past
is stored in an enormous building in England
except a child, maybe that child
who is still watching the boats on the river.

And if that child were my son,
I would put a hand on his shoulder,
point across the river, and tell him
that is where they keep all the time that has ever passed.

And if a daughter, I would do the same thing,
but on the walk home under a row of shade trees
I would probably break down
and admit to her—or even him—that it was just a story

I made up while waiting for someone
in a bar in New York, and because she was so late
she had to sit and listen to the longer version
of how the past is not mere concept

or a realm we have never occupied
any more than we will ever occupy the future,
but rather a thing of extraordinary size
salted away in a massive power station.

Where are the snows of yesteryear?
Where have all the flowers gone?
And the lightfoot lads and the rose-lipped maidens?
Across the flowing river in that big building made of brick.

Richard Howard

Taken for a Ride

I cannot come to the phone. Please record your message.
Richard? *Richard!* The queerest thing—only
That's *not* what you'd call the *mot juste*, is it?
Okay, the *strangest* thing just happened . . . strange
             to *me* in any case, and
I've got to tell you what I—no, *ask you*
what I should do with it—I mean, maybe
I ought to show the damn thing to the cops?
             I've got to do *something*, but
you're not home, or you're just *not answering*
for some reason, maybe somebody's there,
is that it? But before *I* do anything
             you've got to know what *he* did,
I mean, this *person.* Who else could I mean?
He sat down right across the car from me
—on the Broadway Express, the longest stretch
             between stations, Times Square to
Seventy-Second, not a soul around—
did I say it was late? Well it was late,
no one was around . . . Oh, maybe there was
             someone at the other end,
someone fast asleep, but no one watching,
actually looking at the two of us,
not the way *he* was looking at *me*, not
             just looking, *staring through me*
and not smiling—frowning! Concentrating
on something *inside me*, that's what I thought
at first, until I realized it was
             inside him, and when I looked

away, looked down, *there It was* all right,
free and clear, ready and waiting for me,
or for anyone who had the right *effect*,
                    I mean, there was no fumbling
with his fly or fidgeting to get It out
of his—could there have been underwear?
Not a clue: It was just *there*, big as life,
                    nor was he *playing with It*—
what a ridiculous expression! This
was dead serious: no need to touch It
or help It along in any way . . . Richard,
                    It didn't need any help—
and I think that's what I resented most.
After all, I wasn't exactly shocked,
I've seen more of those—and at closer range—
                    than you've had meals. But I was
dismayed: *he* wasn't looking at me—*It* was!
And I think most women, even the ones
unaccustomed to such exhibitions,
                    are put off by the solo
bow, the detached battery, as if
in fact it was merely an attachment—
who can get *attached* to an *attachment?*
                    Maybe you men (I mean *gay men*)
manage better because you already
possess such a thing—*prepossession!*
Anyway, all he was up for (to speak
                    plainly) was spectator sports,
apparently all that was . . . required.
                    We must have been at least
past Lincoln Center by then, and . . . nothing!
That was my moment of inspiration.
I had my new cell phone out, just checking
                    which number to call in case
anything bad happened, and then it came
to me, you know? I was as well-prepared
as he was for this *looking* business:
                    what you see is what you get,
so I set the damn lens without a glance
and snapped three shots of him—and of *It!*—

Before he realized what I had done,
             almost before *I* realized . . .
And then I stood up—*It* was still standing,
free and clear, as I said. I wonder if
a woman *ever* has much to do with
             the fruits of such *posturing!*
It all seemed to be happening to him
—and to *It*—without my involvement
or (saving my uncertain presence) need.
             So what am I, *chopped liver?*
Anyway, there I stood, and as the train
pulled into the station, I just held up my
little cellphone camera so he could see
             the last picture (mostly *It*)
and smiled and walked out the opening doors
onto the platform and up the stairs and
into the Rose Bar I'm calling you from . . .
             Perhaps you'd like me to print
out the three little shots of him (and his
Keepsake) for your own purposes? You might
be pleased with the Sacred Image, you might
             even have enjoyed the show . . .
Funny to think that when every briefcase
and baby-carriage is liable to be
inspected for concealed . . . weaponry, such
             Perilous appendages
can be tacitly worn and openly
deployed. The Way We Live Now: explosives
forbidden unless displayed. As all the signs
on our university doors announce:
             YOU MUST SHOW ID TO ENTER.
Who's the wiser—who comes off best? The police,
for another nutcase; my showman, for
a passing release from his compulsion;
             or me, for turning him in?
Richard, you have to deci . . .

This machine cannot record any further messages.

B. H. Fairchild

The Church of the New Jerusalem, Pawnee Rock, Kansas

North across the tracks and past the fallen GANO
in a gaggle of shacks and collapsing farm homes
huddled in their groves of wind breaks, the church
of Immanuel Swedenborg shoulders live oak branches
ancient as the tribes of Kansas or the sorrow notes
of thrumming fence wire and blesses with the spirit
of William Blake's unlettered wife the wracked,
abandoned husks of tractors, doorless pickups,
and the odd, half-buried hearse in someone's long
backyard gone to cheatgrass and rusted oil cans
across the road.
        Catherine Blake walks the crumbling
WPA sidewalks through the diminished town,
and her husband's dark and fallen seraphim
are mare's tails in the pearl-gray skies of dusk.
She was the midwife of Blake's illuminations,
and when one year later they escaped the Church
of the New Jerusalem, he prophesied that heaven
and hell would marry, his demons and Swedenborg's
too lucid cherubs embracing in an ecstasy of love
and irony.
        Without contraries is no progression,
the disappearing town of Pawnee Rock rigid
in its long descent into the unforgiving past.
MAGNETO ELECTRIC leans against the closed P.O.
and on the west GARY'S AUTO SERVICE lets the wind
keen and rasp through half-boarded windows.

In Catherine's thrift shop at closing time
the angels of memory inhabit every garment
to enter once again the streets of commerce,
rich Saturdays of trade and barter, Mennonites
in black wagons where towheads gawked
and mouthed in redneck wonder the songs
of innocence, the old men on the corner spitting
Red Man and unravelling tales of better days and
shrewder men, land cleared and furrowed, boasting
rain follows the plow, the dream that came undone.

We share the bumper of my car to sit and watch
the congregation of eleven leaving Swedenborg's
basilica. *Hippies*, she says. *They come in on a bus*,
the cry of the faithful lifted now in loud goodbyes
as the bus rumbles out cloaked in yellow dust.

And this is visionary Kansas: the last believers
plunged back into a night where the angels
of a Lutheran engineer rise above Wal-Mart
and the corporate fields of chemicals and wheat.
And two hard skeptics speak into the hollow streets
of vanishing, the emptiness that follows ruin,
the vagrant ways of memory and mental flight,
and the garments that clothed the backs
of women who, like her, signed their names
carefully with an X and saw the New Jerusalem
in a vision real as the land could give
and then slowly take away, false as prophecy.

The Gray Man

We are cutting weeds and sunflowers on the shoulder,
the gray man and I, red dust coiling up around us,
muddying our sweat-smeared mugs, clogging our hair,
the iron heel of an August Kansas sun pushing down
on the scythes we raise against it and swing down
in an almost homicidal rage and drunken weariness.
And I keep my distance. He's a new hire just off
the highway, a hitchhiker sick to death of hunger,
the cruelties of the road, and our boss hates
poverty just enough to hire it, even this old man,
a dead, leaden pall upon his skin so vile it makes you
pull away, the gray trousers and state-issue black
prison boots, the bloodless, grim, unmoving lips,
and the eyes set in concrete, dark hallways that lead
to darker rooms down somewhere in the basement
of the soul's despair. Two weeks. He hasn't said
a word. *He's a goddamned ghost*, I tell my father.
Light flashes from his scythe as he decapitates
big clumps of yellow blooms, a flailing, brutal war
against the lords of labor, I suppose, against the state,
the world, himself, who knows. When we break,
I watch the canteen's water bleed from the corners
of his mouth, a spreading wound across his shirt,
the way he spits into the swollen pile of blue stem
and rank bindweed as if he hates it and everything
that grows, a hatred that has roots and thickens,
twisting, snarled around itself. A lizard wanders
into sunlight, and he hacks at it, chopping clods
until dust clouds rise like mist around him, and then
he speaks in a kind of shattering of glass cutting
through the hot wind's sigh, the fear: *Love thine enemy*.
He says it to the weeds or maybe what they stand for.
Then, knees buckling, with a rasping, gutted sob
as if drowning in that slough of dirty air, he begins,
trembling, to cry.

        I was a boy. The plains wind
leaned against the uncut weeds. High wires hummed
with human voices in their travail. And the highway
I had worked but never traveled lay across the fields
and vanished in that distant gray where day meets night.

Jason Bredle

Apocalypse

If eating corndogs and watching the demo-
lition derby on TNN
Friday nights is a sign of the apocalypse,
then the end of the world is certainly being birthed
in my living room. But I shouldn't run away from it
like actors from computer simulated dinosaurs,
instead I should welcome it with open
arms and a smile, take it home and give it
a name—Ted or Julio. After all, it needs
love and acceptance just like anyone.
Think about it, how would you feel if everyone
feared your impending arrival? If Steve
tried to disguise his voice whenever you called
and everyone on the camping trip sat around
the campfire drinking hot beer, trying
to get so drunk they wouldn't notice
your presence? You'd feel pretty rotten,
wouldn't you? So I'm saying, don't
abandon the apocalypse at Tony's house
in Pittsburgh and get a ticket while speeding away
in Zanesville, Ohio. I mean, Tony's
no child caregiver, he's an auto mechanic
for Christ's sake—he'll fix your Toyota but not
your life. Give it some time to grow, you'll
realize everything will have been worthwhile.
By junior high it'll be going steady with girls,
playing Strat-O-Matic baseball every
Tuesday, shoving the heads of unsuspecting
nerds into toilet bowls. You'll see, by

high school it'll be dating a cheerleader
named Crystal and be captain of the football team.
It'll finally get that metallic blue Firebird
working. It'll graduate, go to business
college, flunk out, get a job
at the alignment place west of town, spray
paint Crystal Hudson's name on an overpass
just before she leaves it for a guy who repairs
small engines at Rick's Small Engine
Repair. It'll spend its nights on the back porch
drinking Wild Turkey and Old Milwaukee,
pining for the good old days. Pretty
soon everything will begin to fall apart—
it'll be buying more and more shotguns
and stashing them in the closet, talking about
our right to bear arms. It'll start saying
backwoods militia groups make a lot of sense.
That's when everything will go down. You'll
be sitting around one afternoon
watching Mama's Family because it's on
Channel 2 and Channel 2 is the only
channel you get, and everything prophesied
will erupt. Most will die. And you'll be one
of the last remaining, driving down I-64
in a white Toronado, turning the radio
to AM 1610 for some
information—weather, tourism, fishing,
you won't care. You'll be searching for an off track
wagering facility to put 500 dollars
down on inescapable death and end up
at a British Petroleum in Burnt Prairie, Illinois,
refueling and cleaning your windshield in silence,
a Ford Aerostar on either side of you
filled with men staring at you, mumbling
to one another in Spanish.

The Year of Living Regrettably

That was the year the woman you loved
left you standing alone in a Wal-Mart
parking lot, the year you spent in central
Mexico, the year you saw too much
of I-70 after midnight and highway 46
after three, the year of ten thousand deaths,
the year clouds rose so high
and the sky became so yellow you thought
this must be the end, this has to be
the end—but it wasn't, and each morning
you'd wake at 5:30 and drive
from Bloomington to Indianapolis to survey
the damage, the housing communities destroyed,
the trees uprooted and everyone still alive
after all these years. Today is Rosetta
Lee Southerland Pippenger's one hundredth
birthday and she doesn't know any
of this. Lord knows she's lived on a farm
outside Grubbs, Arkansas with her family
most of her life. She doesn't even know
what Bloomington in early March feels like,
the sky so dark and the wind emerging from so
far overhead, then falling downward toward
South Walnut where you walk amongst
the traffic and the people moving this way
and that, marrying, forming bands, practicing
in the basement. It's like this feeling, this desire
to get in your car and drive to Louisville and keep
going until you've forgotten everything
that's ever happened, everything you've ever
known—that summer you dragged Sarah's
dog up from the road and buried him,
that summer you asked her to marry you
in Knoxville, that summer she won't remember
because of you, but because of the guy
she left you for, that summer was hot wasn't it,

and you'd only know later it'd be the dog's
last. Rosetta Lee Southerland Pippenger has 21
grandchildren, 45 great-grandchildren,
and 41 great-great-grandchildren.
Yes, that's quite a bit of procreation,
though I bet she never found herself sitting
on Laura's bathroom floor one Halloween
in Chicago amidst the lime green frog decor
thinking dear God, I've got to think
of a way out of this mess, I don't belong here.
A danceable melody, maybe. I've never
told anyone this, but I almost couldn't
take it anymore the night of the prom,
her sequined dress and beautiful hair
and insistence that I didn't love her
were too much to handle. It was prom
night for God's sake and Jennifer Wilson
had eaten my raspberry tort without asking.
This is visiting your hometown for a week,
this is longing to be back in that mess,
before the ice has melted and the swans
have returned, before the summer people
come back with their aquatic apparatuses
and custom vans. This is a balcony, heat
and sitting beside the Ohio River with someone
you love, listening to her laugh at the name
of a bizarre refreshment. This is driving to Ypsilanti
to visit Anne, this is a wrathful God,
this is what we go through, the owls at three
in the morning, the deer looking at you through
the front window, your mother and father asleep
upstairs in their separate rooms. This is eating
too much Mexican food and spending an entire
evening trying to recover. This is falling
asleep in the park every day before
delivering newspapers or eating Korean
food. This is blueness, then greenness,
a choreographed step, a glass of wine,
and finally, in the end, erupting into a rage
and walking out of a bar around two AM.

This is waking from a dream and scribbling
I'm living on a houseboat—a dog keeps
asking me if I want to play some jazz
improv, I wake up, I'm in my childhood
bed. I have two twin beds I can push
together if you want to come over. Dear Dave,
I've finally found that place, that place to buy
athletic shoes without being hassled by failed
track and field stars in referee jerseys, where
they actually have your size and the salesmen
don't come back out with two
boxes saying well, we've got a size
four and a size eighteen, sometimes they run
a little big you know so these babies
might fit you but there's no way
a shoe eight sizes too small
is going to fit you and shoe buying has always
been so horrible hasn't it, because in junior
high if you only owned one pair
of shoes you got hassled for it by guys named
Ron or Shane who would be football stars
for the moment but by the time you'd graduated
high school it seemed like they'd become
dust and escaped through the ventilation system,
out into the world where we all breathe Rons
and Shanes every day, which may be why
we're sometimes cruel even when
we don't want to be, why we may get
upset at two in the morning in Detroit and why
we yell at people we love over the phone
when they tell us they never want to speak
to us again, and why they tell us they never
want to speak to us again. All you know
is someone is crying and now is not the time
to have a conversation about a prewar
Britain. Right now I wonder if Rosetta
Lee Southerland Pippenger has ever been
in a sewing club, ever discussed true
left handed knitting at a local bookstore
while you and I leaf through books

about people named Doug and Carly, and right
now I doubt she's ever participated
in an egg tossing competition in a swimsuit
or had a gallon of ice dumped on her while
lounging beside the Pacific Ocean. And the feeling
of walking out of that bookstore is so
wonderful, the yellowness of the street lighting
so close to perfect, so close
to perfect—like resting on the couch on a spring
afternoon, the windows open, the raccoon down
by the rowboat and your cat beside you, eyes
closed—never wanting the moment to end.
The place you once called home, the place
you felt most comfortable, the place you loved
Sarah and lost and loved again is now the one
place that seems foreign to you. It's like driving
north on I-69 on a Friday afternoon
and noticing a sign that says FOR TRAFFIC INFO,
TURN TO 530 AM, not seeing
any traffic and turning on the radio
only to hear someone talking about you.

Denise Duhamel

Lucky Me

I've written two novels for adults and one for teens,
none of which were published with covers, artwork on the front
and blurbs on the back. They never were put on bookshelves
in libraries or in stores, never assigned a price or a barcode,
never marked down or remaindered. I never signed a copy
or had someone come up to me to say, "Hey, I'm in the middle
of your novel—not bad." The titles were *Precious Blood, That Song
You Know the One about Love,* and *It was Long Ago and Far Away.* Wait,
there is also a third adult novel in there somewhere, the second
one I wrote—I can't even remember the title. Each took me
over a year to finish. And there was a screenplay
called *Headlines,* a comedy about a weather girl in New York
and her crazy brother who wants to become famous, but he has no real
    talent
and is not a murderer or a winning pie-eating contestant
so he's pretty much screwed. I wrote that screenplay with Jim Fall
who was more a director than a writer, though he was extremely funny
with dialogue and had a great collection of movie posters and
    soundtracks—
when we got stuck in our plot, we'd get up and dance. Jim is gay
and his music was mostly disco even though we wrote our screenplay
in the late 80s. He later worked for Dolly Parton's production company
and let me Xerox copies of *Precious Blood* in Dolly's office,
on Dolly's dime. (I'm sorry, Dolly! I really thought the book
would sell and then there'd be a screenplay that Jim and I would write
and you'd have a big part and compose a song called "Precious Blood"
for the soundtrack and that was how I was going to pay you back.)
Jim went on to direct *Trick*—a great movie—and he's directing
now for TV. I went on to write *Pickles,* another screenplay, this one

about a mother and daughter who are accepted to college the same
    year
and even live in the same dorm. The mother gave up the daughter
who was adopted by another family—and the two figure out slowly
that they are related because they're in the same biology class.
This was a comedy too, or so I thought. My friend read it
and he said it made him laugh, even though the jokes were a little
    broad
and there were a few logic problems. I tried to fix them,
but the more I read it, the more *Pickles* didn't quite make sense.
Jim had a sugar daddy we were convinced would finance *Headlines,*
but their relationship fell apart, and *Headlines* was never made
or even optioned—otherwise I wouldn't be writing about it with such
    nostalgia
and regret. Our agent lived on the Lower East Side near me.
She was really into ecology. You couldn't flush paper down her toilet—
you put it in a covered bucket next to her trashcan.
This totally embarrassed me. I never quite understood
why it was less harmful to the environment to throw toilet paper away
rather than flush it. Her toilet paper was grainy—biodegradable, I
    guess.
She kept having us revise *Headlines* and, at one point, pulled me aside
and told me that maybe I should write a sample script for *Cheers*
or a new show she thought I'd like called *Roseanne*. I'd never seen
    Cheers,
but I wrote two *Roseanne* scripts, one having to do with D.J.
mauling Barbie dolls and another one about Roseanne having a crush
on Johnny Cash. Later there was an episode about Roseanne
having a thing for Wayne Newton, but I'd obviously picked the wrong
    celebrity
and never was hired. I also wrote a few episodes of *She* TV, a vehicle
for my friend who was a stand-up comic and wanted to be a VJ on
    VH1,
but they told her she didn't have big enough boobs. She used to
    jokingly say,
"Just tell me who to blow to get this job and I'll do it . . ." a joke I
    tried to use, too,
but by then I was mostly writing poetry and the joke fell flat,
the joke teller (me) more pathetic because she was just trying
to get published in tiny literary magazines with a print run of 200

rather than make hundreds of thousands of dollars. My stand-up
    comic friend
believed in me and my poetry. She was the one who got me addicted
to coffee (iced coffee with milk) from the donut shop on 23rd Street
and Eighth Avenue. I never liked coffee until I was 25 or 26
and that was one of the ways I stayed a kid as long as I could. I also
    wrote
a few skits for *Wake Up, Jerusalem* for another friend who was also
    trying
to break into comedy or acting. But I didn't understand enough about
    Jewish
culture, so my punch lines were always a little bit off. I was typecast
in real life as the kooky best friend to women who would later go on to
    play
the kooky best friend in movies or TV. Laura played Hal's best friend
    in *Shallow*
Hal, and Mindy went on to play a schoolmarm in a Woody Allen movie.
And I was always just that far removed, my nose so close I could sniff
each celebrity walk by. In 1986, I actually met Kevin Bacon at a party
for *Quicksilver*, his bicycle messenger movie. My friend Michael was an
    assistant
to a talent agent and would get us tickets to go to events where we
    could eat
cold salmon and fancy cheeses for free. Kevin probably knew
    Quicksilver
was going to be a flop, but still he was upbeat and kind. He asked me
    what I did
for a living and I told him that I was a writer, which was stretching it
since at that point I was in grad school and teaching comp.
    "Screenplays?"
he asked, with what seemed like genuine interest. But Jim and I hadn't
    started
Headlines yet, so I said, "No, I'm a poet . . ." at which point he drifted
    away.
A few years earlier I'd met Julia Roberts at a party for *Star 80*
at Eric Roberts' apartment. Michael said, "Mark my words—
she is going to be the next big thing." I talked to Julia for a while
and told Michael he was crazy. She was mousy. Her teeth seemed
much smaller, less white back then—I don't remember any kind of
    flashy smile.

Her hair was that color that wasn't blond or brown
and she seemed, well, dull. I predicted Madonna was a flash in the
    pan—
Cyndi Lauper was the real singer, a star with staying power.
I was proven wrong over and over again. And although now I say,
"Wow! Lucky me, I get to live and breathe poetry . . ."
for a while I hated myself for not making it in prose—with movie
    rights
and screen credits and meetings with stars and walk on parts.
Maybe, Michael says, I simply wasn't hungry enough.
But I know I was famished. I remember eating one particularly
    delicious lunch
at my Bank of America temp desk—
soda crackers and seedless grapes
I'd lifted at a party for Liza Minnelli
nestled in paper napkins at the bottom of my Goodwill purse.

October 1973

When Mrs. Dubois knocked on the side door and said, "Girls, stay where you are. Your mother is on her way home," I knew Grammy was dead.

I was thirteen, my sister twelve. We'd felt so grown up coming home from school on our own, remembering our keys and taking in the mail. Our father wouldn't be back from work for a few hours and our plan was to do our homework to Jim Croce full blast then set the table. Our mother was "away," gone to a place where she could "rest." Before she left, she'd been listening to her Johnny Mathis albums on the same record player in the living room, the one with the gold diamond pattern on the front speakers and sliding doors on top to keep the dust away from the turntable. Except when my mother listed to Johnny, she didn't do homework or anything productive—instead, she'd sob into the couch cushions leaving tiny mascara smudges.

Before my mother went away, Grammy said, "If you leave, I'll swallow all my pills."

My mother snapped, "Don't let me stop you!" because my grandmother had threatened suicide so many times.

At least once a week, my mother had abandoned her dinner midway to speed to Grammy's to try to talk her out of it. Once she even took her to have her stomach pumped. Grammy'd spent time in the hospital with the duck pond, which reminded me of the place Billie Holiday went to in *Lady Sings the Blues*, a book I wasn't supposed to read, but couldn't put down. Grammy didn't use heroin, just Valium. She and my mother traded pills like Necco wafers at the kitchen table, no gardenias in their hair or glamorous careers. When Grammy had shock treatments, my mother cried afterwards that her mother looked like burnt toast.

"Grammy's not dead," my sister said. "You're being dramatic. Mom probably just missed us and wants to come home."

But I knew this wasn't true—our mother wouldn't miss us. Once when I threatened to run away, my mother said, matter-of-factly, that she was thinking about it too. The little hairs on my arms stood at attention as my mother kept stirring whatever it was she was making in a silver bowl. Besides, I had seen sadness in Mrs. Dubois' face, that same sadness she had when the hearse came up her steep driveway to take away her son. I knew Grammy was gone.

My sister and I straightened up. We made sure the kitchen counter wasn't sticky—the offense my mother hated most of all.

When my mother came through the door, she stood clutching her light blue suitcase, unable to put it down, unable perhaps to admit that she was home and that her mother was dead and here were two daughters who needed her. My sister clung to her waist and started to cry. I pried her fingers from the handle—it wasn't easy. I pulled at the sleeves of her cardigan until it was off.

I made her a highball with the vodka she kept on the highest shelf and a can of ginger ale I'd just opened for myself.

I think I said, "It's not your fault."

My mother asked, "How did you know where my vodka was?"

Dean Young

Lives of the Vanishing Flying Aces

It was said he'd written pornographic plays
under an assumed cloak of indifference
initially in French, a tongue he found
in a steamer trunk. At the peak of his fame
he enflamed his admirers by going electric
which turned out only to create more fans
infuriatingly of the robotic sort, good only
for circulating air. Mostly he liked shopping
unrecognized except for the few who knew
the secret signal, a waiter or two,
the woman who'd cut his hair so long
she'd be invaluable to the reconstruction
of his skull. He boasted of drinking wolf milk
not often enough and those that answered
his questionnaire found him viviparous,
prone to stalling snits. Remember
that dust-up with the Supreme Court
about his trash, whose was it really
and what did it reveal? Suddenly
we all felt unmasked by our own rubbish,
a new entertainment scuffling our disbelief.
Also poo-poo'ed was the unified self
which helped explain why we couldn't find
our cars in the parking structure
and in the post-parking structure
of free floating referents. No one
was anyone. No one was getting pregnant
then everyone was pregnant, except whales,
there were fewer and fewer of them around.

Rex hung new storms on the summer cottage
but Meg wished the sum had been spent
on her horse who died without a monument.
Earl proved an inadequate liar
and that compounded his surgical failures.
More and more, we missed Jimmy Carter.
50 was the new pink, 40 the new gray, hello
the new goodbye, Vancouver the new Paris,
meat the new bread. That homeless guy
who convinced us he could read Greek
and looked too much like your old man
one day was gone, just his rug left
then that too vanished after a couple rains.
Then the great obliterating snows came,
first a speedy doodle then a Victorian novel.
Edith and Edwin were finally hitched.
A new satellite was launched, privately.
Some things came out in the hiring process
that couldn't be put back like a joke snake
out of a fake can of nuts magically
made real enough to bite the birthday boy
but nothing a sprinkled cupcake couldn't cure.
The search for a replacement was stifled
by the original's refusal to shuffle off
and no one wanted that, too much like
a second date with your ex-wife.
You tried to keep up with her dad though,
the widowed flyboy retiree who preserved
a spectral hum in his dim afternoons,
a hobby of diorama bombing raids.
He was the last of his squadron
and the only person he ever loved
had become a cloud, some days nimbus,
others serious but always what he'd gladly
vanish in if only it'd come down
now that he was grounded.

Articles of Faith

I used to like Nicole Kidman
now I like Kirsten Dunst.
Jennifer Aniston is a schmuck
and Brad's sure a rotter
even if I was the only one who liked him in *Troy*
he had the Achillian pout right.
I much prefer the *Creature of the Black Lagoon*'s environmental
    warning
to the Invisible Man's exploration of neurosis
although in the update with Kevin Bacon
I liked the nudity.
When it says at the bottom in small print
language, gore and nudity
I like that
but the Sisterhood of the Traveling Pants
made me cry on an airplane
got to be the lack of cabin pressure.
Grown men should not wear shorts in airports
unless they're baggage handlers.
Bearded men should never play the flute.
Most heavy metal music is anger over repressed homoerotic urges
is the sort of idea that got me beat up in high school.
There is nothing sadder than a leaf
falling from a tree then catching an updraft higher than the tree
then getting stuck in a gutter.
Symbolism is highly suspicious because it can't be helped.
There is always something you can never touch, never have
but there it is, right in front of you.
The opposite is also true.
Even though the bells are ringing
your glissando is private.
Truth labors to keep up with the tabloids.
Every word is a euphemism.
Every accident is organized by a secret system
and you're telling me life isn't personal?
The starfish disgorges its stomach to devour its prey.

A network of deceptions festoons the cortege.

An exacto knife cuts the kingfisher from an ad.

In the beginning the divine creator wrote 999 words and created 999
demigods to translate each word into 999 words and 999 angels to
translate each translated word into 999 words and 999 exalted
priests to translate each translated word of the translated words into
999 words and we are an error in one of those words.

Vows exchanged in an aerodrome.

Ovals without consequence.

Masterpiece wrapping paper.

The hurricane makes of homes exploded brains.

Central Intelligence Agency.

The early explorers were extremely agitated men, anti-social, violent,
prone to drink.

Demons walk the earth.

Says so on a tee shirt.

We are born defenseless.

It's a miracle.

Hey Baby

You had reached into the dark hole
but the theogony was gone. Then
there was a shout and the movie broke.
Only the robot monkeys could move
and they had only a couple hours left
in their batteries, the same current event
had been running for years, exchequers
prowling in assault vehicles looking for
just the sort of person to beat the shit out of
I was but no way was I doing their job
for them, least not so you could tell
from my permanent record. I controlled myself
on remote. I had a free sub coming.
I wasn't interested in the movie
but the dark was proving exceptional
except for the clichéd screaming.
I longed for my garage. The rag
that had its face pushed in many accidents,
the bicycle hung upside down like an attempt
to rehabilitate an instrument of torture,
the interior decorated by bats.
When I'm dead I'll reach up and pull
some hot chick down by her legs
into my pupa and make a baby.
Baby will build me a monument
and not just some pile of junk either.
Small, expensive replicas will be available
in the battlefield gift shop.

Cate Marvin

Little Poem That Tries

Little Poem That Tries likes to make pretend it is a land
where dislikes inform its borders, tells its knees to leave
if they won't stop kneeling, then announces it's time to

my Kentucky courthouse heart my credit counseling heart

clean house. Its orders come from the top, shudder their
way down, striking fear into the bowels of the lowliest
custodial workers. Appoints serial killers for its customs

my file for bankruptcy heart my long distance phone call

officials. Destroys its orange groves with a single dream.
Reenters the house, limping. Acquires an endless supply
of Xanax, believes it possible it is living inside a movie

heart my courtesy call heart my manual dial I am dying

and when the sun calms down—if the fervent sun ever
calms itself down—it'll pat itself on the back, think how
much prettier the days are with the companion of a sun

heart my note in my throat tries and dies heart my Jersey

that kills: how in drought graves split open, cannot keep
their bones down. The land's heated disarray underneath
such violet skies; does it not remind one of a tangled sheet,

Turnpike heart my Divorce Court heart my small claims

how the pill of the past is easy enough to swallow once
it's crushed up, spoon-fed with this: such amorous light?
To gaze all day as the sun plays along a riot of graves . . .

heart my service window heart my claimant heart my

rather a peaceful pastime, as if what's been said is truly
done. Though it never intended to undertake a coup, one
might conclude from the teary countenances of officials

hit my car heart my notarized heart my foreclosed heart

round the conference table that the Little Poem That Tries
was never right for this job in the first place. After it pats
its reader down, it slips into a hired car, makes itself *far,*

my unsubsidized loan heart my on loan and lonely heart

makes itself *away*. Now, the hot, purpling sky turns to fog.
All the scorched fields shrink below. The still stars above.
And Little Poem That Tries snows and snows and snows.

my how could you have hit the one nice thing I owned heart

Poem That Wears Your Scarf

knows my milky neck as I stand street-cornered,
rivering one last look at you back toward my iris.
Market bouquets jut fierce heads out the collars
of their paper cones. Everywhere the signs appall:
Fresh Cut Flowers, the violet blooms heralding
dismay I am moving toward you in this peopled
square. Even at this distance, the two blue disks
set in your head conduct their hypnosis, revolve
like pinwheels, pale twins that spin me epileptic.
My eyes dark as wish-coins tossed to fade slowly
into the murk at a fountain's bottom, your eyes
so light they look lighter than ice, a pale closer
to nothing than any iris I've seen: as the distilled
clarity of a drink looks weak and yet is stronger
than one might think. Your eyes that did me in.

It begins again with you, succulent darling, your
mouth pressing so hard at mine our teeth *clack*.
All kisses should be so onomatopoetic, all love
should be loud enough to scare off the neighbors.
We put the reds of our tongues to bed, tuck them
deep in the jewelry boxes of our mouths. Falling
from out the doorway hinged to a strange man's
house to land on the peculiar glittering of asphalt
at 5 A.M., a new sun so diamond and inexplicable
shuddering up brick walls. The taxi was waiting
around the corner, but we didn't notice the corner.
Why was it taking so long? We will never sleep
again. Days later, on a train heading south, your
head falls, perches itself like a boulder on the sharp
edge of my shoulder. I sneeze blood into a napkin.

Did you know I liked how our bodies flinched?
Your bed tight with ice covers, never a place for
lovers. Your floors slick and fogged, set as still
and hard as the face of an opaque lake. Branches

outside clacking in wind, everywhere a glittering.
The slow syrup of chilled vodka sliding its arctic
snake down my throat. How nights trembled, seal
entrails wetting snow darkly, just-clubbed, while
disco lights revolved all around us, us emptying
drinks into our mouths as criminals shake stolen
purses out, dump their contents into black sacks.
How even the air there was muzzled. I loved being
locked in the walk-in freezer of your apartment
where you fed me paté and chardonnay, allowed
me to watch you sleep. *I love you,* I told the wall.

Moments before the streets will wrap their scarves
around our necks and I will cast my stare out from
the window set at the cab's back, avenues rivering
opalescent behind us, and we step out, oily rainbows
puddling round our boot-heels, I am walking alone.
I do not know your very pale eyes yet. Can I not
sense my desire, as I move languid beneath sun cast
on the sidewalk, for your brand of decadence? *No.*
I will lie in your bed, watch as you peel an orange.
I will allow my mouth to open, let in your fingers.
I lose my hat, I lose my mittens, I lose my head.
When the blizzard hits, all is white, and you stand
me before a mirror, wind your scarf round my neck.
Now I want to push this story down your throat.
I see you cornered on the street corner. I approach.

Phyllis Moore

Why I Hate Martin Frobisher

Because he says I look like Deborah Kerr
Because he leaves wet towels on the bedspread
Because all mothers, waitresses, and bank ladies love him on the spot
Because he wears T-shirts with girls on them
Because he never gets parking tickets
Because he never breaks the Sorrento wineglasses
Because when he's mad we duke it out, and when I'm mad I need to
    calm down
Because he looks at me when I reach for the Land O' Lakes unsalted
    when Breakstone's on sale for a dollar fifty a pound
Because he watches sports on TV
Because he works and I just read books
Because when I'm screaming like an oceanliner, he can answer the
    phone and say, "Sure, no problem"
Because my mother thinks he's the spotty pup and I'm Cruella
    de Vil
Because he plays with his food, cuts curliques into my 4-hour
    crème brûlée
Because he's always wrong and I'm the first to say sorry
Because he tries to placate me

Because he buys generic fabric softener instead of Downy
Because he does not want to go to the Red Party and gives me a
    15-Watt excuse and we do not go to the Red Party
Because when he's stupid I'm too tired to point it out and when
    I'm stupid he's all there
Because he strains to hear *All Things Considered* when I'm biting
    his ankles

Because when I'm weepy and refuse to get out of the car it's time
        for the shrink, but when he puts his fist through my grand-
        mother's bevelled mirror he's just getting things out
Because he's glued to The MacNeil/Lehrer Report while I preview
        my upcoming suicide
Because he never trips me up

Because he made me his grandmother
Because he notices waterspots on the glassware but hasn't an
        inkling about the man I've been sleeping with for over a
        year
Because he's so unlayered he doesn't know when I'm being mean
Because he no longer puts notes in my pockets for me to find
        later at the office by the Mr. Coffee machine
Because he no longer reads me to sleep from One Thousand and
        One Arabian Nights

Because in front of the judge he looks like Clark Gable and I look
        like the stepmother
Because he's got a heart the size of a chipped acorn, the brains
        of a squirrel, he's a jerk,
        a little girl's blouse,
        a felon, but straight-seamed,
        a cream-faced, two-penny
        scoundrel and a kitten kicker,
        a real badass and
        I want him back, oh yeah.

Charles Harper Webb

Jackass: The Viewer

Why do I remember *Jackass: the Movie* when so much
has gushed from the cracked crankcase of my mind?
My brain has dumped the words King Lear howled

on the heath, but saved the Fool promising some car-
rental guy, "I'll take good care of this baby," then driving
straight to Demolition Derby. I've fuzzed the year

of William's Conquest, but see clearly the car crumpled
like a paper-wad, the same Fool claiming, "It was like this
when I got it." I can't recall women I've slept with,

or forget Sir Wastebasket-Head pedaling his bike
through a grocery store, push-broom lance scattering canned
goods as he falls. I can't define *Bauhaus,* but recall

the industrial-strength moron who paper-cut his own tongue,
then begged to be shot with a bean-bag gun, screamed,
wriggled, writhed on the floor, and later showed off

a black and purple bruise big as a fist. Paying the phone
bill slips my mind, but not "Bungee Jump Wedgie."
Brains save what they think they need to survive—

not Nobel Prize economics, but "Ass Kicked by a [Karate
Champion] Girl." I barely smile watching that French
mime What's-His-Name, but nearly fill my pantaloons

watching a guy crack a newspaper in a hardware store,
then deflower the display commode. I can't contain
the sense of *teleology*, but can't let go of sqwonking

air-horns as pro putters flail. I can't quote one line
of Hart Crane, or grasp why celebrated critics celebrate
certain poets of today, but I remember the dwarf

(Wee Man) who high-kicked his own head, then strolled
down a jammed street under a red traffic cone as rivers
of heedless Japanese flowed by. I can't recall my wife's

birthday, but can't forget the limo-shape in the X-ray
of that imbecile who shoved a toy car where the sun
don't want to go. I draw a blank on *tenth birthday*,

though I know my parents spent a mint on mine; yet
I remember "Alligator Tightrope"'s dolt-with-a-dead-
chicken-in-his-shorts, and Señor Business Suit washing-

machined down two city blocks by "Tidal Wave."
Why is High Culture so hard to grasp today?
Why is History so easily displaced? Is my life a waste

because I can't recite the periodic table, or Boyle's Law,
or the first bars of Beethoven's Ninth, or my password
to the *Times* online archives, or how many cups

in a gallon, or my city councilman (if I have one),
or my state senator or national representative, or how
to take square roots, or who won the Battle of Bull Run,

or the difference between Lope de Vega and Cabeza
de Vaca, or exactly why my ex filed on me, but
I remember the white guy in Tokyo who snorted hot

wasabi until he threw up. His fellow diners seemed
incredulous at first, then laughed so hard that one bent down
and threw up too.

Everybody Tries So Hard

Even slackers and no-accounts, bobbing and weaving
    away from work. Even bums, perfecting looks
of misery, hands like goose-heads snapping up
    cash by the freeway overpass. The bald man
mounting his wife tries so hard, sweat on his pate,
    his buttocks pumping, the tense, serious little pud
swollen with purpose, puffing, "I think I can,"
    his partner straining to get through this, eyes squinched

shut in what (good worker!) she hopes is ecstasy,
    trying so hard to focus on one glowing spot,
the little man-in-a-boat rowing so hard to finish
    and go home. Everyone tries; and every *thing*—
the squirrels that have plenty of nuts, but keep on
    packing their fat cheeks, saving, saving—the pigeons
that flap so hard to get their corn-fed bodies off
    the ground when Timmy runs up with his dog, trying

for a mouth-full of feathers, a hand-full of flight—
    the steel propellers in Johnny Rocket's silver cans
spinning like mad to mix ice cream, chocolate, and milk
    into a malt human livers bust their trusses to digest,
consumers straining to believe they're still wasp-waisted,
    seventeen, life opening like a field of golden poppies
just ahead. It's touching, sexy; it infarcts my heart
    how hard they try. The convict who broke his back

to duck *responsibility* (his dad's favorite word)
    as if it were a smart bomb homing on his head—
now, in jail, he slaves to steal fruit he can mix
    with Jello, sugar packets, syrup, Lord knows
what, and store it all in plastic bags he risks his life
    to swipe, and brew in them the putrid *Pruno*
fellow cons struggle to like, trying to rouse a decent
    drunk, trying so hard, like thousands of breast-feeding

women who march on the capitol, panting, sweating,
    lugging babies furrow-faced with concentration,
baby-mouths frantic to feed brains that will spend
    their lives fighting to get ahead like those Kentucky
farmers who gave their all to grow tobacco
    until the klieg light of the public's eye, the furnace
of the courts' indignation turned on them, millions
    of lawyers—sweaty, rubbed raw by law school—

trying so hard to make their hard trying pay off.
    As writs, statutes, subpoenas fell like stogie-chomping
locusts on the fields of Marlboro and Pall Mall,
    the farmers tried to keep their farms afloat, blowing
for all they were worth into Tradition's leaky
    water-wings before clambering aboard the lifeboat
of B & B Worm Farms, whose salesmen promised
    easy money raising worms for agriculture, worms

for industry—worms by the billions boring
    through compost, leaving "castings" to make
bumper crops a cinch—worms that would do all
    the hard work, breeding, eating, casting off fortunes
in feces while the farmers could finally buy a new
    truck, fly to Aruba, get some peace, some R & R,
never dreaming B & B would be the biggest
    pyramid scam in Kentucky history, its owner

dying, leaving these farmers who tried so hard
    with barns stuffed full of worthless worms—millions
of dollars blown on worms who tried their best
    to find enough food in the earth they ate to keep
hearts beating, bodies wriggling when the farmers,
    gone bust, abandoned them, the compost drying
with all the worms still fighting to digest the dust
    that wouldn't feed them, however hard they tried.

Adrian Blevins

Semantic Relations

Though naturally I love them, they are a monstrosity, acute and unruly,
already pigheaded on the way from the airport to come and infect me

with what kind of mayonnaise is better than Hellmann's and which
    of us
got the new bike versus who crashed the old and who's drinking too
    much

versus who ought to get the special Weight-Watchers brownies
and who isn't on that plan but really should be and whose kid is in
    what university

versus whose kid is in which other. Yes I love them but they
talk too much about nothing because they are after pulling me out of
    the stillness

I came up North for because in their opinion I've always been too
    faraway
starting in the 1970s like an anonymous planet up in my room

while they all sat around downstairs vehement on the topic
of everything I was missing because after all it was *just* the hearth—

just the kids pouring juice and telling jokes while the scant one
    upstairs
plotted some wraithlike escape like could she become some kind of
    particle?

Could she float out to sea maybe on a raft of splintered pillars?
This is part of the story of my people who won't say much

but rigorously chatter about global warming and formaldehyde and
    cancer
and Hemingway and Peter Jennings and Bush who we despise

because he is a killer. My people are not killers—they are romantics—
they like to sit around on porches and tell false stories because lies

are more agreeable than me eyeing them haughtily and saying
as a matter of fact, though I'm forced to do it because we're almost out

of time, o my high-hilled, prattling sweethearts—o my brothers and
    sisters
of hoodwink and swindle and fiddle and twaddle and drivel and
    hokum and tripe.

Sin City

I've got to know everything or I'll fail as a person, so of course I
  watched
the Triple X DVD with my husband, who's jumbo-electric-frenetic-
  feral
even when he's trying to stop me from wasting money on the
  telephone's Star-69 feature

because I am altogether lethargy and he's up at dawn even on the
  weekends
because he is the reincarnation of the founding fathers
and I won't even mop the kitchen floor during the weeks he's flying all
  over the country

making a ton of money I admit I merrily use for murky purposes like
  Ritz dye,
which is good for changing an off-blue jacket into a burgundy one,
which is good for whiling the time away while he's gone making all
  that money

I'd make myself if someone would just hire me, though in addition to
  being lazy
I'm so crazy I take out my heart and measure it with a plastic green
  ruler,
and, while he's grilling kabobs and installing dimmer switches and
  tasting the garden soil

to gauge how much pH must be added, announce suddenly in the
  garage,
where in addition to grilling he's designing a workbench and an opera
  for Martin guitars,
that I am *megawatts* in The Benevolence Category

because if there's one thing I won't do it's make the same mistake
  twice,
referring to the divorce, and for this reason I'll watch *Sin City*
  with him,
though he's got to promise the kids won't catch us and answer any
  question I posit

regarding the erections of the cameramen and the pain of the putting
  in of the clit rings.
But now I can't stop worrying about Delray of the ceramic bowl breasts
that could not move to accommodate Brick's tongue, which I'm
  guessing

from the look of that sugar-white scar must have been slashed all-but-
  in-half
by the inmate who must've taught him that pitiless thump-thump-
  thumping trick
I fear will infect Delray's insides with a malignancy that will cause her
  eggs to rupture

and her poor Mama to die forlorn in a nursing home from the lack of
  baby slaver and baby cluck
that is the only viable hereafter if you are a sinner like she is a sinner
  and I am a sinner,
though God knows this time I'm giving virtue a shot.

The Theater People

As I remember, they were enormous, like countless cymbals striking,
each one in sickly separation the whole show itself coming through
    the door

with me as nothing but epidermis in the tub back when I'm nine
    or ten
bathing during my parents' parties while eyeing the pink robe on the
    iron hook

since the actors, playwrights, poets, painters, & windfall ass-biters
would always have to pee or vomit or put the lid down & smoke
    a joint

& take a breather, I remember they'd say, while I'd fill up my
    two palms
& drink the tap water as hot as it would come since I guess that was
    my medicine

against how much they loathed the war & Phyllis Schlafly &
    Richard Nixon
& each other if they were breaking up or themselves if they were
    drunk,

which they were, for I remember tumblers & I remember stumbling:
    I remember
jingling at the wrists & stretched-out black eyelashes & somehow-
    hectic Capri pants

because even if that wasn't really Anne Sexton in my bathroom
    swallowing pâté
so she could throw it all up so the pants would fit the next day, it
    always was

Anne Sexton & Dylan Thomas & their vaporous faces in there
calling me *little girl* & weeping & mumbling & shivering & shaking

until I'd stand up & dry off & stroke their swollen hands until they
   were
enormous again downstairs with the others singing loud enough

to wake a far-flung neighborhood. Don't wonder why or if the
   propensity
swelled to other years in other rooms & kinds & types of sticky death.

This is about the paltry heart that must get gutted sometimes &
   knotted
& lit-up while sodden. It makes no difference to a story how ample is
   our fury.

Stephen Dunn

The Key To

    Think about it, the wrong answer
is money, though that room
with a balcony overlooking the Aegean
will, for a while, make you believe
otherwise.

      But not if you're with X
whose sense of a view never turns
inward, or with Y, all politics and soul,
who can't relax amidst splendor.

    Ah, but with Z, she of the beautiful
ambivalences, how interesting to move
this way and then that—the odd comfort,
the thrill of it.

        Another wrong answer is power,
which wants itself again and again,
though with Z you can imagine
needing just enough of it to have something

          to renounce. Her hesitations,
the way she worries each word
into usage, everything about her
asks you to dig a little deeper

        into what's sexy, what isn't,
whereas X doesn't understand
how you can be at a local bar,
holding her hand, and at the same moment

elsewhere, say Morocco,
in a cave with gypsies. Y understands,
but lets her feelings about the Third World
interfere with her lovemaking.

Half in,
half out, that's for Z one reasonable way
of *being here*. You could spend a lifetime
looking for a woman like that. One of you,
for once, shouldn't think twice.

Cecilia Llompart

The Lord's Prayer

Our Father, Who art in the gleam of polished silverware.
In the indigo smudge exposed, between layers of dust,
when we swipe a gloved finger across the sky. In pupils
as they widen. In the blood and breezes. In tongues that
swell purple with words and in the gaping mouths of fish.

Hallowed be the broken aria of the clouds. Choir that angels
would sell their wings to join. Trumpet Yourself into the
tender coil of our ears not so much with velocity, or smothered
between commercial breaks: But with more plunk. And
more ripple. Like the rusty acoustics of a playground, or
the dry scrape of ceramic bowls ushered around a dinner table.

Thy Kingdom slip from the salty grip of stagehands to
drop and jerk on cables like some plump marionette.
But draw the curtains apart slowly. Let us rouge our
cheeks before your coming, oh escort to the upper room.
Deus ex machina, dangling stiff and pigeon-toed.

Thy Will be cradled in the softest arms. Unbuttoned and put
to sleep between plastic dolls. Be mopped off floors. Sewn
into our collars with a size and a note to see reverse for care.
Cut into portions the size of parables and pierced with
toothpicks. Taken with bread, with wine. Like bread. Like wine.

Give us this day our daily flask. Our daily fossil exhibit.
Our daily holocaust survivor. Our daily tickertape parade.
The headlines in bold and a daily puddle to soak them in.
May we never count our blessings before they hatch. May
there always be the other cheek. May we bleed internally.

And forgive us our secrets. Our silence. Our scabs.
The way the wind rubs itself against us until we grieve
with it. The way we make time go by faster by closing
one eye. Slower, by crossing two arms. Forgive every
thing we store in Ziploc bags and freeze overnight.

As we forgive those who refuse to believe in the buzz of
their own green dreams. Those who lick their fingertips and
pinch flames out instead of letting wax be wax. As we forgive
those who hold a finger up to puckered lips and demonstrate
how to deflate. Who store the future on the highest shelf.

Lead us not up and down aisle after supermarket aisle,
confections to cut your teeth on, to put a crack in every
smile. You squint and it blurs for miles. Roads more
traveled by. Towns with lean, mispronounceable street
names. Between rocks and other hard places. Lead us
not into the lion's den unless the exit sign is lit within.

But deliver us from ourselves. From digital watches.
From gargling clichés before bed. From casting pearls,
or worse, stringing them. Stuffing our pockets. Deliver
us from paradise and, whatever coy tree grows there,
from biting into apple after apple after apple after apple.

For Thine are the clenched teeth and the broken taillights.
Are the branches that droop with their over zealous fruit
blistering to nourish the soil, while over ripened bellies
plead through lips of cracked clay for twenty cents a day.

Forever and ever times infinity. Amen.

Bob Hicok

The Bible Is Explained

32   And lo, your Bibles shall be made
of the thinnest paper, such that turning
the page of My Word, a crinkly wind
shall bluster about the ears
of the congregation, making you believe
My Spirit has entered your church
through the stained glass windows,
that I have come to bless
your stiff shoes and superfluous hats.
33   And you shall be made to say
the word "and" all the hours of the day,
and the word "so" shall trail behind
the word "and," and the word "for"
shall follow in the shadow of "so,"
34   and your Bibles shall be scented
with anaphora so that you may practice
repeating things, and the sound "behold"
shall burn on your tongue, and you shall think,
does he mean the furniture polish, and I do not,
though I have nothing against the glow
of the dining room table.
35   And you shall forget most
of what I have said, and come to understand
that I did not speak most of what is claimed
for My mouth,
36   for would God have intoned,
"And next to them Meremoth the son of Uriah,
the son of Hakkoz made repairs.
And next to him Meshullam the son of Berechiah

the son of Meshezabel made repairs.
And next to him Zadok the son of Baana
also made repairs," I mean, who are these people,
what is this falling down place?
37   And you shall wonder about the politics
of the Twenty Seven Books, and the Gospel
of Judas shall enter the sun,
and you shall howl yes and you shall howl no,
and you shall see in the miracle of the tree,
in the rising up of rivers to the sky,
that I need not have bothered with dictation,
that language is the least of My touch.
38   And you shall prick your veins
with poppies, with the wonder of the field,
and you shall lie down a dove and rise
a snake, and you shall think a mushroom
into the clouds, and burn My throne with war,
39   and I shall forgive your forgettings,
your vanities, if you come to see that the Bible
is but a seed-case around these words,
40   "And just as you want men to treat you,
treat them the same," that I have encased the Truth
with stories to keep you entertained,
41   so you may know your only purpose
is to love each other, that if you do not
I shall smite thee—is it smite or smote?—
that is just the way I am, get over it,
and you shall return to the Earth,
and the Earth shall return to its star,
and its star shall return to the Nothing
from which all stars came,
42   and it shall be quiet, and I shall finally
get some reading done, and I shall miss you
in the way a dog misses its fleas,
in the way the wind misses the dust
it has worn,
43   and I shall try again, only this time,
among your endless cousins, I shall dispense my Word
but not a single tongue.

Gabriel Gudding

[Athinam Nagaram Katam]

Athinam nagaram katam,
mamsalohitalepanam.
Yattha jara ca maccu ca,
mano makkho ca ohito.

Here is a citadel built of bones,
plastered with flesh and blood,
wherein are concealed decay,
death, vanity and deceit.

—Dhammapada, 150

Because basically we are bathwater in a bag. And these knuckles are
pink rotatable pebbles, and our pecs are slabs of blood-stuffed foam. And
because a child is again rushing up the scene of joy.

Because your mother's buttocks have been sunlit. And because yes we
want to believe frogs and bees are noble but if Barbie and Mrs. Hermby
are not noble then of course a frog is neither. And a frog is a malformed
meat flower. Delicate like genital meat but, too, a kind of pus-blossom.
It is a ditch jewel. A globule of the slatch. A cross between a grasshop-
per and a blister. Indeed a frog is a snake's kitten.

Because shit now look, I have maimed my hands on the microscope and
now the little world is bloody. Because my body is a bag that gives me
this feeling, that feeling.

Because the spanking of children is still practiced in this realm of
hearses.

Because without the example of insects, Ovid could not have written
the *Metamorphoses*.

Because the peacock's fan is to adorn its sphincter. Or to camouflage it.

And because what has passed through our bodies but artery rope, dried semen shortcake so buttly beef, the semen treacle trailing in the tracks of its rills, the bloody cold booby sherbet, her mulches of mucus mayonnaised on skin flake fishfood, and there was the nipple pizza, the sphincter calzone, her pus tea, the colon candy of her feces, her warm poop manna, the baby's cartilage mutton, the turkey-like clitoris chowder, the eyelid mincemeat, the man's highball of crudens, her grandpa's nectar of catarrh, the hospital's bulbs of hymen sausage, we hiked forever through sputum sherry downed with earlobe stew, the eyebrow hair-bread before cupcakes of foreskin, that tepid swig of sweat with a little blood tea and Jello of menses, that jujube of jejunum was delish after the scrotum goulash, esophagus salami, testicle custard, adenoids caviar, smegma fondues, and we kept hiking through the perineum brisket, the golden urine sherbets, biscuits of eyelash, those labia on the bagels, your mother's breast milk milkshake, her poop corn—her hams indeed of poop, her booby half-n-half, and, too, the smell of the pyres in your sister's beaten anus: flashes, conflagrations; the sheet-fire in her pants, the tornado of her yammy calories, the blazes, the flames, the hard banging of flames through the hot funk of roasting
in the hut
of her butt. A caloric, pyrectic collection of brown and fiery candle-bombs that came from your sister. And too the brown loaf forming in each of us like an umber stalactite or some bronze tawny trout over-cresting our inner buttocks waterfall. The post-meat trout introrse—acroatic and acroamatic: the brown-visored banker of our feces banker.

And because we are here in this realm of bladders: with our dental problems, under this stupid hair, our toes jammed in little turbans of fungus.

Because my nose is a kind of dual vagina. I might root around there on occasion and bring out an olden baby of mucus, or a young pipe of mucus. This latter mucus might spill around in a baggy manner, like a teat of liquor—the color and shape of a small bag of pear liqueur.

Because we are here in this, with our daughters, with our joys and the fears.

Because in the Arctic, of course, the human being is the only disgusting thing for miles. But not so in Mississippi!

Because the pitying of humpbacks is sweet, the pitying of harelips tender, but that bald men have often been pitied.

Because I have a salt cake made from the pee of your brother. Because you found your laugh in a dime store.

Because that clammy bolt had held up the empire, you puss. Because we pulled it from your brother's hmmhmm.

Because the snorkel is a prosthetic throat.

And because yes we removed the Bausch microscope from your aunt's bathroom and it had fecal stains on the eyepiece.

Because a pig is essentially a pachydermic dog.

Because a bee is a kind of duck among insects. And worry is a brick carried by the wind of anxiety. Because still there are babies in the prairies, delicate as boiled objects, whom mothers have lost, all of it patrolled by flies dressed in raisin bodies.

And the dense satellites go on clanging in the firmament. Like peregrine clams. And the weight of bones in our feet. Does not stop us from walking. All the teeth from our town's jaws. Will be scattered to the corn.

And so we are here still, each day, in this parliament of Natashas, our boobies packed into beds, until we rise to go in our sitting, to the end, the strand, the cul de sac, of this unavoidable sorrowing.

Because this ape-stream of nutriment, crafted into boobies and drama, may yet be crossed, may yet be clogged, bunged, choked, blocked, may yet be jammed, arrested, braked, stopped, stopped up and stemmed. And we may walk, in fact we skip, we walk, we run, we jog, we sail as in a boat, or as in a courac, we sail as in a skiff, to sit to the end of this sorrow.

[And What, Friends, Is a Sea]

And what, friends, is called a ship? If there is, friends, any kind of large vessel, subject to be steered for the purposes of moving a range of items over seawater, this vessel being composed of various materials—whether metal or wood, concrete or fiberglass—such that it floats, carrying objects one wishes to keep dry—this, friends, is called a ship.

And what, friends, is called a sea? If there is, friends, an expanse of seawater, positioned between continents or amid various nations, such that it may be coated by pointy waves, supportive of various kinds of wind—whether gusts or light breeze, whether slight breeze or gentle breeze, whether moderate breeze or fresh breeze, strong breeze or gale, whether moderate gale or fresh gale, strong gale or whole gale, or whether wind storm or hooricane—this wind being usually clear or grey, resembling an invisible rack from which various birds may be suspended—any such expanse of seawater providing a relatively frictionless surface for the purposes of sea travel, a surface one may study but not understand, at which one may stare but not comprehend, and whose bottom is constituted by shells, muds, corals, sands, trenches or volcanic elements—being thus a more or less *gargantuan* body of seawater inclined to induce humility in those adjacent to it or poised upon it, which humility may itself come in the guise of awe, vomiting, or tourism—this, friends, is a called a sea.

And what, friends, is called a cruise? If there is an activity, friends, constituted by the unilateral movement of several hundred people en masse across the surface of seawater, aboard a ship engaged in the approximation of a hotel, in which one may find the selling of jewelry, clothing, alcohol, and a diversity of commemorative objects, and upon which the days are divided by a person called a "cruise director," whose name may be Dave, and whose voice piercingly comes unbidden through the various ceilings of the ship, the days thus being divided by the cruise director into group activities whose purpose is to render controlled approximations of joy, which are called "fun"—this, friends, is called a cruise.

And what, friends, is called a friend? If there are, friends, any kind of companions, with whom one shares this joy or that joy, and who at times can aid one in the often difficult task of retaining the capacity to be surprised by this life, and with whom one feels fortunate to have spent time, even a little time, whether eating dinner or writing poetry, whether talking of Tristan Tzara or staring at the wake of a ship—even a little time talking of frigate birds or chatting with the children of these companions or engaging in small talks by a street bench on a tiny is-land—any such person toward whom one is inclined to feel gratitude for having shared, even briefly, the endless humility of this life—this, friends, is called a friend.

Richard Cecil

Communication

Thank god for cell phones! Now I can talk
while walking by myself but not draw stares
from people passing by me on the street,
since one of every two or three lone walkers
shouts to an invisible companion.
But still I keep my voice down when I say,
"Sweet Kitties!" to my absent cats, now dead—
a habit I took up when they moved in
twenty years ago and started acting
so cute all day and night that I praised them
even when they weren't there to listen.
"Pretty kitties, darling kitty cats,"
I whisper like the Pope's ejaculations,
which have indulgencies attached to them:
"Blessed Virgin Mary Pray for Us,"
"Lord Have Mercy on My Sins," etc.
Each repetition cuts the sinner's sentence
by fifty days or so in Purgatory.
Once in fifth grade I logged a hundred years
of time off my to-be-determined sentence.
But constant praying drowned out all my thoughts,
and so I bombed the quiz in long division
and got a sixty on the spelling test.
And, besides, all of my sins were Mortal,
which meant I'd spend eternity in Hell,
"from which there is no possible reprieve,"
according to the Catholic Catechism.
Forever minus a century's forever—
that's the math I fully understood.

What I needed was a Plenary Indulgence,
the kind that popes sold in the middle ages,
where the buyer's soul is cleansed of all its sins
and its sentence to be roasted is commuted.
But since the Reformation you can't buy those;
in modern times the only way to earn
a Plenary Indulgence is martyrdom.
So I stopped muttering ejaculations
except for cheers and curses—"Holy Shit!"
But still I couldn't seem to keep my mouth shut.
I had to talk, if only to myself,
which got me into trouble in the classroom
until I got promoted to professor,
where doing all the talking is encouraged
by students who refuse to raise their hands—
though they're the ones who, filing out of class,
instantly dial up their friends to chat
on their way to the dining hall or dorm.
I let them get two steps ahead, then call
out to my absent cats—"Oh, you darlings"—
the way I used to when they waited for me,
listening for my footsteps on the porch.
Now they're somewhere I can only reach
by talking to myself. "Sweet kitty cats"
re-conjures them for me just for a second:
hungry and meowing by the door,
knowing that I'm coming home to feed them.
"What would you kitties like to eat for supper?"
I whisper as I pass a girl who's weeping
into her cell phone. The kitties say, "thin air."

Sharon Olds

Near Boys' Prep

There's something that I do, every night,
the boy in the bus seat next to me said,
quite loud, to his friend. *I jack off, and I do it*
the good way. He was maybe twelve,
and his friend, eleven, said, *I'm happy*
for you, though I thought, like me, he would have liked
to know what the good way was. *How many*
hairs do you have, at a certain point?
twelve asked, and eleven replied, *At a certain*
point—on my head—I have uncountable
hairs. On my other side, a young
man of about sixteen sat down,
and his handsome friend leaned over us and asked him,
If she would, would you, with Rebecca? No,
said the seated one, *Would you? No . . . It's like—*
"*Jean, can I touch your breasts?*" then a falsetto
squeak, "*No!*" "*Sorry; Mary,*
can I touch your breasts?" "*No!*" "*Sorry;*
Naomi, can I touch your breasts?" "*No!*"
"*Sorry; Betsy, can I touch your breasts?*"
"*No!*" He rained this down on us,
baritone and squeal—it was, in its way,
funny, though I felt near tears, as if sitting
beneath contempt. And I remembered times
I had rhapsodized about my children
with someone who did not have children,
times I had tried to describe my love
for my husband to someone alone. How daunting
the human is, how we use our hour of radiance.

Meoluc

Meoluc, meole, mlicht, blicht,
milzti, mrjati, my mother, in the oldest
age she reached, was afraid they might ask her
to live without it—*white or yellowish*
secreted fluid consisting of globules of
fat suspended inside a solution of
casein, sugar, and inorganic
salts. It pleases me to learn
that a substance something like what mountains are made of
came out of my mom's rich molehills, it
delights me that in whole, and in skim,
and in butter, and condensed, and cream, and whey
there is ash—and sometimes, I think, maybe
dust. And the ingredients
for baby teeth came through the nipple
in tiny wisdom molecules.
My mother did not fear her mother
as I feared my mother—she hated her,
so I was not my ma'am's twin, not her
Pollux Milquetoast, though she was Castor
oil enough for me. And as she aged
she feared the doctors were going to command her
to give up the icy lactation taken
from a servant class so low they did not wear
clothes or go to church, and their hooves
stepped in their own shit like a forced
dance in hell. But the product of
the udder, the bovine stand-in for her mother,
brought her one of the strongest pleasures
of her early cronehood—she never got
to have a dotage, so never in her life did she
have to go without the icy
fresh Io froth of her first and
last beloved beverage,
mile, milch, miluh, mjolk,
miluks, μέλγàs, melk, mulgere—cold milk.

Dorianne Laux

A Short History of the Apple

> The crunch is the thing, a certain joy in crashing through
> living tissue, a memory of Neanderthal days.
>
> Edward Bunyard, *The Anatomy of Dessert,* 1929

Teeth at the skin. Anticipation.
Then flesh. Grain on the tongue.
Eve's knees ground in the dirt
Of paradise. Newton watching
Gravity happen. The history
Of apples in every starry core,
Each papery chamber's bright
Bitter seed. Woody stem stump
An infant tree. William Tell
And his lucky arrow. Orchards
Of the Fertile Crescent. Bushels.
Fire blight. Scab and powdery mildew.
Cedar apple rust. The apple endures.
Born of the wild rose, of crab ancestors.
The first pip raised in Kazakhstan.
Snow White with poison on her lips.
The buried blades of Halloween.
Budding and grafting. John Chapman
In his tin pot hat. Oh Westward
Expansion. Apple pie. American
As. Hard cider. Winter banana.
Melt-in-the-mouth made sweet
By hives of Britain's honeybees:
White man's flies. O eat. O eat.

Jynne Dilling Martin

A New Path Will Bring Rich Rewards

Make no mistake about it, slime molds are
the most interesting organisms on Earth.

Chop one's body into little orange pieces
and strew it throughout a labyrinth:

the chunks actually find one another, slither
back together, reclump and glop their way out!

Why not take a page from their book, folks?
Our homogeneity is becoming alarming:

a dutiful child with shined shoes arrives
every thirty minutes for a pianoforte lesson,

the awkward herd in the women's room
take a simultaneous piss at intermission,

we all seem to sit on our asses, look up
at bright things exploding in the sky,

give no thought to sleeping upside-down,
to shooting ourselves in both shoulders,

or to living full-time under the sea! Christ
tried to set a creative example: he was like

hey, here's a bunch of crazy things to try,
you can even put nails through your hands

and end up totally cool in just three days.
But two millennia later, no one even

lives on the moon. He must be disappointed.
Without eyes, wheels, hammers, or phone lines

slime molds have transcended vastly more
challenging circumstances; if they had brains

as well as a sense of humor we'd be the punchline
of every lame-ass slime mold joke. How many

humans does it take to figure out regeneration?
Dunno Bob, shall we sprout fingers to count?

You Are Going to Have Some New Clothes

Do you moan about in a slipshod robe and curl-papers all day,
or click open your pencil case and scratch at pointless arithmetic?
Are you the sort who lies on voluntarily taken personality quizzes,

or do you insist that the deli man slice off thin, nearly invisible, ham,
and do you place said ham in a labeled Meat Drawer of your
    refrigerator?
Thought so. I confess I cannot remember why or when we learned

to live in this manner but I wonder each morning how to start over.
One champion poker player stares continuously into bright lights,
thereby contracting his pupils so his anxiety becomes inscrutable

but I'd like to take that one step further. Amnesia seems delightful
doesn't it? But how to clonk one's self sufficiently, without risking
    coma,
not to mention whether health insurance covers such things—

surely a sympathetic local Allstate agent would process such a claim,
in neat blue cursive write *client hoping to forget normative socialization,
fear of crowds & entire wasted past, baseball bat to head.*

Then when you emerge from her tidy vacuumed office onto the street
what surprising light and color and noise. You will recognize no one,
and each time a word gets shouted, you can choose: run or laugh away.

Rodney Jones

On Fiction

To enjoy a story I have to put myself in the protagonist's shoes—
        literally—as if
for the instant of the telling, I have become the ideal podiatrist,
        and I expect
real scenes—a stable at a hunt club or a Kwik Mart by an overpass—
and actual people with cowlicks or neck braces, even if they
        shortly will defy gravity
or experience multiple orgasms of such proportions as to wipe out
        audits and biopsies.
I want, too, an account of useless virtues, and eccentrics—
        perhaps
a hermit amnesiac with an altruistic streak or an intelligent leader.
Tension goes without saying, a fact like temperament,
        politics, or humidity,
which people die from every day, but that usually must avoid
        direct telling
else we have on our hands a prospectus, dissertation, or treatise.
        Not a story in any event.
A story needs description and dialogue, those mutually parasitic
        engines of attention.
Given language, the story tells itself. But take language back,
you have the loneliness of the author, a quantity one must depart
        in the middle of the night
and travel from tentatively by a series of unanticipated detours
        through a whiteout blizzard.
One friend wore a stocking over his head, seated in his basement
        like a mad
stockcar driver with a yellow sheet rolling onto the platen
        (it had to be yellow)

of an old manual Underwood. Sweating the generative sound,
        he left commas for later drafts.
Another wrote at Denny's on a legal pad (white not yellow). He liked
        having
around him the companionable irrelevant chatter. He wanted
        to live in the world
not out of it, and also to attain the feeling the extraordinary person
        most relishes:
to know unexceptional people with names like Betty or Dot,
        who still need
stories and will tell them without saying a word—a few people,
        professionals mainly,
claim that the story has died, but most people, if they listened,
        would know that, in order
for the story to die with any significant style, time must stop passing.

Sook

Nothing more casual than a cow.
A stained sweatshirt for eyes.
Mud-lathed, scuffmarked hocks.
A breathing, edible log.
Unassuming. Unprepossessed.
Bossy. The constable
tail swishing flies takes
no note signing
the pie-plop behind.
Sublime nonchalance.
A browsing and musing
on the verge of sleep.
Then annoyance after a nap.
A put-upon nun.
No jazz in those horns.
A cast die for the grass in its extrusion to milk and meat.
Also a covenant maker.
A black Baal smelted of timothy and clover.
A sacrifice penned and driven.
A bondage. An acropolis. Her language
does not sound like but means moo
or leave me alone or come
hither calf or holier than
thou. Cow. Corn, her Judas and chocolate.

Deathly

I am alone, driving through St. Louis,
listening to a ballad by Aimee Mann.
There is a fine romance to listening to loud rock 'n roll
as you drive a late model car through a big city late at night:
the ordinary nostalgia, with its useless longing,
and then the clearer nostalgia for what never happened:
Februaries in Rio, blind tropical sweethearts,
the last few treaties of the Gore Administration.
It is acceptable for once to be a fool.
It is totally awesome to have come
from Rolla and to be going to Carbondale.
A cool rain has fallen for most of the day
and now the road glitters with that light
that indicates spring and Eros and things going by:
the Hill, Busch Stadium, then Saarinen's arch;
certain parties in 1973, embraces by banisters, day trips;
many times shining. "It is too late," the music says
without coming right out and saying it. "It is hopeless
and it will never again be so beautiful." A girl
once played this very song for me and told me
it made her think of me, a thing that nearly broke my heart,
though, in fact, it was herself she meant.
The singer alone is the subject of the song.
The rest is only love, for which I remain an idiot.
I think of Neruda's mongoose nearly every day.
Of old girlfriends weeping at my funeral.
Of what Keats wrote to Fanny Brawne,
and how much it pleased me, on May 17, to write in a journal:
"Setting words on top of music
is like placing a fat man on a small pony."
But now as I drive, and I am not supposed to be anywhere,
the words raise that girl, and then myself,
exalted, her attention gilding my ego like rain,
until I begin thinking of other women
together in a car late at night, and of my grandmother,
and her friends, humming as they quilted

scraps of guana sacks and overalls,
how they had already drifted away from me,
when I came out of the Holland Tunnel in 1971.
So as I cross the Mississippi, I play it again,
three times, and then again, a beautiful fool
in the ugly age of Bush and Cheney,
alone in the dark country, singing along,
driving with my lights out for the fun of it.

Fat Johnny

Fat Johnny's mom re-nailed the pantry door.
Re-locked the fridge, re-emptied the bread bin,
returned un-nibbled Snickers to the store.
Fat Johnny's on a diet once again.

She checked beneath his bed. The sight was chilling.
Where did the green-fur on the rug begin
to lap the blue fur on the donut filling?
Fat Johnny's on a diet once again.

Mom sighed, and said she'd buy more cottage cheese.
Alone, Fat Johnny slipped into the den.
His stomach fluttered like a hive of bees.
Fat Johnny's on a diet once again.

The sofa yielded Zotz, four TV clickers,
nine un-popped popcorn kernels, one pork skin,
and something that looked, but didn't taste, like Snickers.
Fat Johnny's on a diet once again.

Mom loves how Johnny scrubs the house so clean:
the floors licked bright as they have ever been-
(She wonders why she's low on Vaseline.
A boy can't *chew* a single, dry saltine!)
Fat Johnny's on a diet once again.

Her home's so clean Mom canned the cleaning service.
But Johnny's starving. He has a ravenous yen.
And Minnie the guinea pig is looking nervous.
Fat Johnny's on a diet once again.

The Ice-Cream Truck

From blocks away the music floats
to my enchanted ears.
It builds. It's here! And then it fades—
and I explode in tears.

I kick the TV set, and scream,
sobbing to extort her,
while Mom stares at *One Life to Live*,
and won't give me a quarter.

I pause, change tactics, snatch a coin
from the bottom of her purse,
then race to catch the ice-cream truck,
ignoring Mama's curse.

I stop the truck, I start to choose—
then see I won't be eating.
I stare down at a goddamn dime,
and trudge home to my beating.

Grandmother's Bed

At Grandmother's grave, I stood at her dead feet
and somersaulted up to her dead face.
I wish I'd worn golf shoes. Man, that'd be sweet!

I love to think of her in that cold place
without blankets or night light, and nothing to eat—
with dirt as her pillow and dirt her pillowcase.

Mom sniffled and cried. She said it was sweet
how time, God's love and human forgiveness erase
the pain we'd suffered. What pain? It's a treat

the witch isn't here to hawk snot in the fireplace,
and croak love songs to her damn parakeet.
After she died, I sprayed it with her can of Mace

and laughed as it coughed out one last half-tweet.
It was the only witness that saw me replace
her heart pills with blue pills I bought down the street.

Since her hard heart hiccupped its final beat,
the bed we shared is all mine, though it's cold as concrete
and the stale scent of lavender clings to the sheet.

My Hero

My uncle takes me fishing
and to the picture show,

and when he looks at me
I see his tanned face glow.

Next weekend is the circus,
and I can't wait to go.

He promised me an ice cream—
and an extra Oreo

if I fumble in his pocket
and pull it out real slow.

He asks about my girlfriends
and calls me Romeo—

then winks a naughty wink,
whistles sly and low,

and chuckles when I blush.
He's only kidding though.

I've heard him in the hallway,
walking tippy-toe

and listening at my door.
He thinks that I don't know

he's checking up on me.
He's anguished at my woe

as I've cried myself to sleep
for months. A steady flow

of tears drips off my nose
and soaks my Batman pillow

since he gave me a book
by Edgar Allen Poe.

Why else would he stand there,
trembling in his Speedo?

He says I'll have to wait
another year or so,

so I won't still be sobbing
at bricked-up Fortunato

and Berenice's teeth
scattered to and fro,

but when I go sleep over
with him and his friend Joe,

we'll wear gold briefs and watch
his favorite video!

I'll bet I won't be scared of
The Rocky Horror Show.

The County Fair

I breezed by bumper cars
and past the Ferris wheel
and found the roller coaster
because I love to squeal

as the cars clank slowly upward,
groaning near the top,
before the screaming falters
and—one, two, three—we drop!

From gut to gullet, shudders
trembled through my chest
each time we cleared a peak
and clattered down the crest.

I stopped and ate a snow cone,
a deep-fried Chocolate Swirl
a corn dog, half a pickle—
then rode the Tilt-A-Whirl.

I tilt-a-whirled three times
and roller-coastered four
before I found the sideshows
and started to explore.

I watched a man eat razors,
a lady sawn in half,
the crawfish boy, a dwarf or two,
and one six-legged calf.

I watched a woman strip
to a shiny black silk scrap
before I saw her beard
and upchucked on my lap.

Robert Wrigley

In Camp, After Praising—Too Exactly— His Beloved, the Ass Man Is Rescued by a Falling Star

It is the best way to see the night sky, lying down
      and looking up, though it might also be, what
with the whiskey and not seeing each others' shadowed faces,
      why they all have spoken at length
and with such earnest conviction on the subject
      of the bodies of women. One man's lover's backside, you see,
has come to be the ass at hand, or in the air at least—
      imagined, constellated, appearing as a heavenly roundness
the ancient fearful seers of bears, hunters, and gods
      never seemed to quite make out among the stars.
They've been around, these men. From legs to lips
      to eyes and more, and now in the silence
after this one's psalm, his breathless, impassioned disquisition,
      his inspired shape-making out of syllables,
she herself seems to shimmer there, along with something
      almost like regret, something with the smoke
and whiskey they all can almost taste.
      It was the detail about her tailbone, the rounded
sacral nubbin, off-centered just to the left
      of the furrow between the soft rising swells of her—
and there she is: he has undressed her and knows
      now his old friends cannot stop their minds' eyes from seeing.
He feels ashamed, a little, imagining how they'll look at her,
      knowing, covetous perhaps, some new yearning
in them he'll hear in the silence and believe
      is there. And this is to say nothing of the stars

or of God, Whom the talkative one has forgotten, Whom
      he does not believe in, and Who perhaps could smite him,
this little man among little men, a man
      who, if he believed, would know
God loves him, God loves them all.
      So small and beautiful their dreams, their flawed,
forgettable, pitiful unfaiths. God thinks, why not
      go ahead and send a speck of ice and dust
to score the ancient, metaphorical sky, an erasure,
      and by so doing give the men back their tongues, each one
by name and also by their naming. And let them
      keep talking, He thinks, let them move on,
though not far, toward heaven, and of such miracles as those
      His believers insist He alone has fashioned,
and in such love as they offer—let whatever these men say be prayers.

Polina Barskova
Translated from the Russian by Luba Golburt

Russian Poets in Venice

Guttural wheeze of one poet turns into a guttural wheeze of another
    one. Voices decay.
The gilded mechanical peacock in the Hermitage collection opens/lets
    out his tail

I lie down on the floor of my office, on a rug,
Listening to the old tapes of Brodskii reading his poems:
Every word
Pierces the top of my head as the drop of the Indian ink in the ancient
    torture . . .
There was once time of Bloom.
Now it's time of the Fall.
There was jolly time when arms clanked, when wings rustled . . .
There was time of my quest for Him, time of my awaiting.

Yellow postcards from the damp Piazza of San Marco.
I treasured them so!
I was ready to keep them till the day of Second Coming . . .
Till the day of coming of the guinea pig who lived in the basket
Who had colored beads in his tiny hands. Colored beads from Murano
    lagoon.

I was ready to keep them till the day of my meeting with Tristan
With his magic voice,
With his stinking raw fatal wound.
All my life was about that meeting.
All my life, day after day, minute after minute—
I waited for my Tristan, my black guinea pig;

I looked for him in all the pet-shops.
I didn't want grass-snakes, hedgehogs or canaries!

They didn't find me:
That damp smell from the lagoon.
That moist voice from the Piazza.
They got lost as postcards . . .
One of the postcards had a rare stamp with the gilded peacock.
Another was signed: BEWARE!

I loved both poets with that exhausting love
That ignites you—keeps you alive—and turns you into ashes
So—now I am just ashes. I don't know their names. I don't remember
   their verse.
They are to me like black pearl beads in the dead hands of those who
   sleep on San Michele.

Translated from the Russian by Michael Kunichika

Flipping through Nabokov's
Speak, Memory

Not far from where lies Doctor Kafka,
Where one expects crowds, tourists, souvenirs,
There's nothing but a bench overgrown by emerald ivory.

I'll sit a while and then go.
First left, then right, then straight.
A worn-out cross, a sullen cat, and then a pit.
Some lieutenant, Averchenko, and nearby—the mom

Of one who is beloved by us (by you, by me)
The moisteners of thoughts, who harbor with a shroud
The banal truth of life (they say it's similar to pus)

Here she lies at Prague's outskirts. Alone, the poor thing.
The grave above her's a slattern and ditz.
And sitting above her's a mutt, scratching.

Here she lies at Prague's outskirts, under humid needles.
So dark, so quiet. I fancy: Daphnis and Chloe
Could give themselves over to their delights,
Upon the carpet, fragrant of resin, alive, rusty.

On the outskirts of Prague lies his mother, who
Washed him in the basin, singing.
He thought her then a great tower,
A body of a giant, who into that darkness
Departed, soared, arose; and he but a
Coddled clod, a lump, a ball—
In her hands, a coddled clod, a lump, a ball.

From her hand wafted warmth and home,
At that time, when nowhere could smell of home

For him. Yet even this warmth and charm,
The transparence of her, the hypochondria, French r's,
Like any form of love, finally, bore him.
Nothing remains.

She was dying alone—he couldn't make it,
To go would have been too much, in poor taste.

He remained at his writing table.
The old cat darkly dug around the bits left her.
A bird's round lifeless eye watched him,
And they told him his mother was dead in Prague.

Grief. Grief. Grief. Naked, he's stretched out upon a sheet
Yet she, like a tower, laughs in the heights.
The body of pearls, the body of stars, the body of snow,
Protects him from the words "strangeness" and "terror."

As if it is a window soiled by November rain,
As if you see the birds, the snow, the berries,
And not my melancholic filthy death.

Kim Addonizio

Book Burning

On top of all the copies of Lolita tossed into a parking lot bonfire
    somewhere in Texas
by Bible lovers—how ironic is that, since "bible" means "book," not
    that anyone
who takes the Bible literally is likely to comprehend irony—
along with Humbert Humbert aka Mesmer Mesmer and Dolores *aka*
    Lo *aka* Lola Haze
cruising through the American landscape in ravishing sentences,
along with Henry Miller and all his lovely whores, not to mention
the delicious meals he cadged off his friends while he was broke in
    Paris,
along with Allen Ginsberg ascending chanting over
FIRST BAPTIST GOD IS LOVE BINGO SUPPER SUNDAY
in a column of pink smoke to the tinkling of little Tibetan bells,
and with a bunch of other excellent books some group of spiritually
    impaired Visigoths
deemed inappropriate and corrupt,

there goes the slim paperback my friend Susan and I
relegated to her fireplace last night after drinking too much Sancerre
and saying things like *God I hate this guy's poems* and
Just a single line of Akhmatova is worth his entire smug and trivial oeuvre
and *Do you believe this poser got a Guggenheim,* until *rip* she'd torn the
    cover off
and *tear* there went two pages at once and *crumple* it all burned pretty
    quickly
until we were standing there gleeful and slightly shocked by what we'd
    done

and now this morning I'm thinking of how the ashes of this guy's
   smarmy little imagination
are floating around up there in the ether of magnificent expression
   with Nabokov *et. al.*,
and the bastard's probably thinking
that he deserves to have been sacrificed on the pyre of our ignorance
   and ego,
and is right now looking down and laughing, pitying us and forgiving
   us our folly.

Lawrence Raab

Faithless

> The tide is full, the moon lies fair
> Upon the straits . . .
>
> Matthew Arnold

By mid-July I'm tired of the mountains.
I want to be near the sea,
walk beside it for an hour or two,
watch it cleaning the wounds of the shore.
Such persistence—though we know
there isn't a plan, just this
going back over the same places,
revising everything out.
"Is there a way to win?"
Jane Greer asks Robert Mitchum
in *Out of the Past.* "Well," he says,
"There's a way to lose more slowly."
He knows he shouldn't trust her,
and he doesn't care. Ah, Matthew Arnold,
our lovers are more melancholy than yours,
more desperate, more faithless.
"You can't help anything you do,"
Mitchum tells her at the end.
Which is what he might have told himself.
But nobody ever sees how far
the things we shouldn't feel can take us.
I just want to walk along the shore
for an hour, watch the waves
rearranging whatever they can.
I like the way the sea encourages me

to think about the past,
as if I could leave it where it is:
the moon on the water, the stars
that gleam and are gone.

Nothing There

What would make you happier?
was the question, and I was surprised
24% chose "more meaning in your life,"
as if the problem was how much of it
they didn't have. Of course
they were asking for meaning that helps,
the kind that gives us good reasons
for loss—a child dies, love fades, then friendship,
and soon enough almost everything is gone.

"Why can't we just live terrified
and without consolation?" my friend Stephen said.
"That's how I like it." But I knew
what he really liked was saying it that way,
the little shock of embracing fear, going out to meet
what most of us try hard to avoid. And that
reminded me of the story David used to tell
when we were in college. His car breaks down
or runs out of gas, so he finds himself walking

alone, at night, down an empty road, silence
deepening all around him, and very soon
he's certain he's being followed. He stops,
it stops. To his left: cornfields. And then
quite suddenly he surprises himself
by rushing into them, is surprised even more
when, convinced it's gaining on him, he stops
and turns back, relieved, even happy
to surrender. And of course

it's not there, though that cornfield
must have been spooky enough
in the moonlight, a little breeze
moving the shadows, those papery husks
scraping against each other. In the end,
embarrassment. Then a story. His point

was what you could do to yourself
just by thinking. Or maybe
that wasn't his point. It's been years,

and for reasons I don't understand, perhaps
for no reason at all, our friendship
was set aside, as if nothing had been there
to begin with, the way nothing
was out in that field. Or else
it chose to hide—at the moment
David turned to give himself up—slipping back
into the rows of dry corn, satisfied
to have done whatever it had done.

Campbell McGrath

Dim Sum

If language is a circulatory system of symbols what are images but
    wounds where the blood coagulates as the world's infection rushes
    in?
If consciousness is the subject of the lyric poem, beads of a golden
    abacus calculating a path through time, how do you stop the train
    without derailing it?
If the self is a type of infinite regression are not our attempts to escape
    it, however ingenious, doomed to fail?
Why prefer the cloth of chance to the garment of identity? Why pay
    obeisance to the tyranny of the random?
To discover supra-human creativity one need only consider a cloud, a
    flower, the taste of honey, the sound of constellations turning.
Nature dwarfs our capacities with contemptuous ease, as do the
    Olympian gods and perhaps the Alpha Centaurians gazing down at
    us with pity and disgust,
but if you were to offer me the fruit of their radiant and perfected art I
    would say, so what?
Of course it is sublime, of course it is ineffable—of course they're
    better than us, bathed as they are in rays of harmonic contentment!
Of course we embody oppressive ideologies, of course we are flawed—
    that such easily-confused, thinly-furred,
god-haunted, greed-driven, blood-dazed animals dare to risk the task of
    creation is itself the justification of the act.
Now, what were those dishes Li-Young ordered—chicken feet, tripe,
    whole baby octopus in curry sauce. Delicious!
And for dessert, little cubes of gelatin flavored like coconut, dry and
    woody, and like mango, syrupy and floral, doused in condensed
    milk.
We drink five or six pots of tea and hover perhaps two feet above the

floor watching the voices of the patrons floating around us in the form of Chinese ideograms
the way Bugs Bunny sees cartoon birds and musical notes when struck on the head with a mallet.

Justice

What do you think about there, in that room of fawn and putty wallpaper, blonde wood and green floral upholstery, in the Women's Oncology Center, looking up at the pepper-spackled ceiling tiles, waiting? Do you think, what are the odds? Do you think, we shall persevere, we shall not be deterred? Do you think, we were lucky to get a space so close to Ambulatory Surgery, and the moon above the parking lot in the pre-dawn sky aligned with a single star and fat Venus shining, two good omens? Do you think how much this resembles the morning eight years ago to the month when Jackson was born, or, wait, how many years? Do you think, looking at those around you, that they resemble refugees lined up for soup or Red Cross blankets, that they suggest bundled bodies at the door of some Soviet ministry to beg information, the location of a son, the cause of a wife's disappearance? But what was her crime, Commissar, what was her crime? And still they disappeared, year after year, by the thousands and the millions, into Stalin's unfathomable slaughterhouse. To promulgate death! To surrender to it as we surrender to the bright machinery of hope, the ring of invisible rays that will reveal our fate, the instruments and stoppered vials, latex gloves, floors being mopped and in need of mopping, the nurses' station with its teddy bears and beribboned photographs of high school graduations, doctors gliding silkily past, attendants to the mystery, acolytes gowned in caustic white and surgical green? Do you think, with a smirk, how much this resembles the waiting room at the Toyota dealer as they clean the carbon build-up from the fuel injector system, all the valve jobs and tune-ups to slow the engine's inevitable decline? Do you think how much the worn linoleum reminds you of the North Dade Justice Center, crowds arrayed to receive their fateful dispensation from blunt, impersonal representatives of the system, young women battling obesity lined up for new drivers' licenses, young men straggling into traffic court in flip flops and torn camouflage pants, in gold chains and Snoop Dogg T-shirts, old women dozing in the corners, middle-aged men in service uniforms—janitors, security guards, parking attendants—filling out forms in a version of the language they will never master, a smiling family attired in matching soccer jerseys from the *Selección National de Honduras* waiting for which adjudication to be handed down, which fateful dispensation? Do you feel how powerful a force compassion is, and how to open its floodgates here would be to risk inundation? Do you think, studying the amoeba-shaped plaster patches and water stains on the walls, that the mind resembles an amoeba, pulsing and probing, negotiating obstacles, searching out nutrients? Do you think that the earth is a waiting room from which we shall depart only when summoned by death? *They are ready for you now, Mr. McGrath, please go in.* Do you think, secretly, in the inmost chamber of your being, take them all and spare mine? Take them all into your black dominion, Commissar, even the healthy ones, if so you require, even the visitors reading magazines and the sour-faced children, the fear-stricken mothers and the husbands watching TV—take them all and leave for another day those I love—take even from mine in fair measure if you must, take the ovaries for they have been duly productive, take the uterus for it may be honorably relinquished, take a kidney if it so please you, take from the liver that it may regenerate, take, take, take, leaving only what cannot be spared. Do you think, even the second time the hand grasps your shoulder, that it must be an echo or self-inquisition when that voice begins to speak? *The doctor would like to see you. Please come with me.* And another voice, like a fiery blazon, saying, *The surgery went well. Pathology indicates all the tissue is benign. Your wife is going to be just fine.*

Daniel Borzutzky

Why So Pale and Wan, Fond Lover

Baby, the implication of the explication of the
phenomenon of our attraction is that you have forced me to
adopt this punctilious attitude so as to achieve the
impecunious and vicarious application of my
mouth-mouth on your mouth-mouth. Moreover the fact of our mutual
comprehension permits misdeeds to appear as corrective
measures designed to heighten the paradoxical
sublimation of our bilateral miscommunication.
Baby, let us pause for a moment and reflect. For the voices we
hear in the comfort of our carnage grow faint as we enter
into the joint-stock company of our accidental
fender-bending fornication. For I have seen your face on the
calm and horrible water and I have lick-licked your
inscrutable tongue-tongue in hopes that the impartial hand of
history will furnish further proof that your lip-lip on my
lip-lip might provide the surprising disillusionment of
poetry. For baby I really love your regressive
deterioration and yes baby I really love the
pyramidal fenestration of your suffocating
resuscitation and yes baby I really heart-heart the
ferocious pettiness of your barbarian bonbons for they
make me want to crawl like an eel into the algae of your fat
and furry funhouse. For baby I have sucked the
verisimilitude of your kisser and yes baby I have
nip-nipped the reaction-formation of your post-primitive
libidinal reservoir and yes I have nibbled on the
viviparous snake in the succulent labyrinth of your
inner abyss and yes I have fertilized your amorphous
bundle and yes I have even crawled into the

perpendicular nature of your so-called managerial
enhancement package where I have cried ever so softly to the
evanescent shepherds of your fleshless lover and to the strange
birds playing in your saucy, simmering ambivalence.

The Heart Is a Lonely Perineum

For Anna and Jimmy

And if it is true that all I can do is float
through these tunnels of dust and pain in which
capital swims in the arms of mercilessness,
then I will put you in the coffin I wear
around my waist and bind you with a rose to the
small triangular bone at the end of my
spinal column where the you that is not you shall
meet the you that might be you and together we
will form a family who will flourish inside this
golden abyss whose entryway is guarded by
a gaggle of slithering creditors with
pee-pees for guns and Chinese porcelain for
eyeballs. For who is to say that the air we breathe
is anything more than a secret code both
capricious in structure and marketable in
the substance of its sad and tender humility.
I was teaching the Laotians about the
existential implications of the
conditional voice when a man came on the
loudspeaker and said we were all a bunch of
Mexican widows with secret Jewish husbands
in our titties. A woman in a velvet dress
jumped out of the rosemary bush and showed us
how to hide those we have murdered in our bodies. I
did not know the blind were invisible to
themselves until I chopped up an old harpy, shoved
her into my underpants, and chuckled as she
struggled to put herself back together. Then we
hopped into my Hybrid Honda Civic and sped
across the border to the all-you-can-eat
rotisserie chicken shack whose drive-thru window
clerk is the Virgin Mary on whose lips you must
tap three times before telling her there is a

handful of dust on her posterior vulva
junction, at which point she will become all the
women you should have kissed but didn't. This will come
true, even if you don't believe it.

Carl Dennis

Unsent Letter from the Owner of Fifty-One Summer Street

Now that you've lived for a month
In your new house at 52 Summer,
I thought it might do you good to know
Why you still haven't met me,
Your neighbor across the street,
And why, if I can prevent it, you never will.

I'd like to begin with the solemn promise
The developer made me that nothing
Would ever be built on the spot
Your house now fills completely.
Nothing was to block my view of the hills
That made me feel my life, constricted till then
For reasons I'd rather not go into,
Was open at last to possibility.

I want you to try to imagine the year
I found in the hills my inspiration,
And then the following year I wasted in court
In a vain effort to stop construction.
To listen to all the details so you understand
How deeply your presence wounds me,
Though of course I don't expect you
To put your house on the market and vanish.

I simply want you to realize that your house
Figures in darker plots than the plot of a comedy
Where luck steps forward to solve a housing problem.
I'd like my letter to serve as a cloud
Passing over your house on a sunny day
Long enough to remind you that across the street
It's raining, and somehow you're partly responsible.

Yes, a larger person, writing such words
To vent his disgruntlement, might decide in the end
Not to send them, the wish to protect and pardon
Stronger than the wish to jolt the unknowing.
But try to imagine me as a man
With little interest in being large.

If I hesitate, it won't be a sign
I want to spare you. Only a sign
I don't believe you'll care to listen. No,
You'll shake my words off, I predict, as surely
As I might shake off words equally carping
If I had as little experience of the world
As you are likely to suffer from
And as little interest in gaining more.

Gregory Djanikian

Talking to Myself in the Shower

What fun to recite favorite lines here,
or even the newest recipe for stuffed squash,
the words reverberating in sheets of sound
against the tiles and tympanum.

I've managed to say the Gettysburg Address
in the time it's taken me to shampoo and rinse,
and could there be a better declamation
than the Boy Scout Law, ending as it does
on "clean and reverent," the temple
of the body upright for one more day?

And the conversations I've meant to have:
with the plumber, for instance, whose bills
have resembled Sumerian manuscripts,
indecipherable but for the numbers—
or the mechanic whose "special of the day"
has been to find everything wrong with my car,
his head shaking in sympathy as if to suggest
we are all as damaged as your gasket seals.

And the arguments I've never won—
how deeply satisfying to retrieve them,
drive them home again and again, revised,
refined in the alembic of my imagination
until they gleam.

And all the while, a steady drizzle of rain
on my shoulders, soothing pats on the back
as I stand naked before judge and jury,
both of whom, luckily, happen to be me.

But really, who doesn't long
for a second chance, getting out of the shower
with the fresh soapy odor of redemption,
the droplets of water crowning the head,
the old self, temporarily,
scrubbed down to the new:

now I catch myself in the mirror,
convinced I've never spoken as well
or looked any better than I do,
walking out into the grime

of the day's offenses, ready
for whatever else the world
will throw at me, or whatever
it has held behind, unfinished,
for me to come back to.

Thomas Lux

The Republic of Anesthesia

I don't feel anything today, my country-
men and women, I'm numbed by 21 liters
of Novocain, I feel nothing
from my cowlick to the final ridge of my big toe's nail; my tear
ducts dry-walled, not a sob
or the sigh of an ant left in me, this autumn,
another autumn
in which the world hates itself so much.
Man ties severed head of another man
to the tail of a dog.
One frog eats a smaller frog.
Wisdom teeth, instead of being yanked,
evolve to wisdom fangs.
All day: arid hair-splitting, cheese-paring.
One bank buys another bank
and the little rubber thimble
on the teller's thumb—that stays the same.
Certainly my god
can rip the heart from your god's chest
and will, god willing, with my help.
A trillion milligram hammer,
the arc of its swing
wide as a ring
of Saturn, hits us first
on the right temple
then on the left: *Good night, good night,*
lights out, bark the stars.

Steve Fellner

"Russia is big and so is China"

Overheard statement from President Bush at summit with
Chinese President Hu Jintao

Monopoly is fun and so is strip poker.
The weather is nice and so is this iced tea.
Porcupine quills are sharp and so is that pair of scissors. Be careful,
    OK?
The baby across the aisle from you is loud and so is some rap music.
The GED was hard and so was bungee jumping.
Pink is a color and so is salmon. Salmon is also a fish.
Bruce Willis is still hot and so is Kurt Cobain, though he's dead.
Stoplights are annoying and so are brussels sprouts.
Vitamin C is good for you and so is exercise.
I could stand to lose ten pounds and so could you.
I am lazy and you don't have anywhere else to be.
North Korea is fidgety and so is my little sister. No Ritalin for her.
I am horny and so are most of my dumb friends.
Seven is more than three and so is eight.
The news is strange and so is my hairdresser.
Model airplanes are frustrating and so are summits.
Poisoned Halloween candy is creepy and so is Anthrax.
Used dental floss is icky and so are missiles.
Nuclear weapons are large and so is my penis.
Metaphors are always obvious and so is common sense.
Wisdom is cheap and so is bus fare.
Solar energy is easy and so is my ex-boyfriend Nick.
Armageddon is a bummer and so is Picasso.

I Am Known As Walt Whitman

To the gay men who spend their Friday nights lurking in the cyber
    chat room, I am known
as Walt Whitman. My alias. My secret identity. My better half.
Somewhere in that claim a stupid joke can be found. Don't expect me
to discover it. I'm too busy online looking for the man who offered my
    boyfriend
his first taste of crystal meth. It got him so messed up he couldn't stop
meeting men off the Internet, and then begging them to stay after
    they had their release.
Of course, they always left. Bored, he did other risky things
like having sex in a bathroom stall at Wal-Mart where he was arrested
for indecent exposure. (Somewhere on those tiles there is a trace of
    him.)
He lost his job as a minimum wage-earning bagboy at Wegman's,
    causing him
to avoid the grocery store altogether, the only one in town. Crystal
    kidnaps
your hunger anyway. His appetite resurfaced elsewhere.
Like in orgies where condoms were thought of as unnecessary
    ornaments.
(Somewhere in my voice, useless empathy can be found.) He
    contracted HIV.
I broke up with him because I didn't want to take care of someone
    who was going to die
in such an uninspired way. Somewhere in this narrative
there may be a shred of logic to be found. O, my dumb dead boyfriend,
you are my expired muse. Because I know you gave so kindly to
    strangers, I imagine
your hole as raw as the material for this poem. Bloody and needy and
    lovely. Somewhere in your flesh I
had wished to find a reason to forgive you. Somewhere
in your grave I will find the redemption I'll need for hating you.
Somewhere in another poem I will find the strength to tell this story
without invoking the name of Walt Whitman. But now I need him. I
    need that dead homosexual to find a
way into my prayer for you. I can't let this be a poem about me

and you. It needs to be something larger. Something that moves our
    words
beyond a story of drugs, a memoir of lonely people, a poem of
    catharsis.
Are you listening from the heavens, my worthless love:
Walt Whitman wrote those poems about desire and flesh and never
    felt any better. Somewhere in that
knowledge a lesson can be found. But now
all we have are these words, words which will not be remembered
by any more than a few hungry readers, words which will disappear
as quickly as the instant message in a chat room, words that will be as
    unrecognizable
as the misunderstood ones in what was once someone's meaningless,
    necessary poem.

Margaret Benbow

Evil Twin

You and I stood beneath the sugar tree
I in my white poem veil
and we promised to be good
and to spin a sweet life
from our married silk glands

but your sly little thirsty buddy
dogged us from the cry Go.
His ape smile lurked in the goblin ferns,
his razor tooth snapped our thread.
He digested grain and grape in his boiler gut,
picked his teeth with spikes of grievance,
even snapped up with pleasure
the enemies coming out of his ears. In a year

he was big enough: diablo hoof
kicked down the door. Beware that tongue,
eel of chromium steel. Hide the food money,
iron throat bolts it raw. Bourbon
and Evil Twin are friends for life,
he sees no knife in that golden palm. At night
he howls with the big dogs:
watch that dark horse run.

Evil Twin batters on the window at dawn,
where could his dwelling be? Husband
drives him off to the hills at last,
Fare thee well today. Husband throws roses
on the table at noon. Who could they be for?
Husband tells wife of the Evil Twin,
Forgive every step he took.

Adrian C. Louis

Jesus Finds His Ghost Shirt

Somewhere along the Via Dolorosa
Jesus noticed Mary was AWOL.
Further steps were uncalled for.
His carpenter's heart exploded.
An ejaculation, a quicksilver
burst of evanescence birthed
stars so fragile that tears
seemed quite pointless.
He put down his burden
and went to his car at the curb.
Rummaging around the back seat
he found evidence that made all obvious:
a checkbook, deposits from unknown Johns,
too many rolls of unopened LifeSavers,
plenty of cherry lip balm, and cheap
condoms in tawdry Day-Glo shades.
And, a soft shirt of fringed deerskin
which puzzled him so deeply
that he felt compelled to put it on
and rise from the dead.

Logorrhea

Big city scares. Older I get.
Hey, Murderapolis, MN, too
much shit going down, walk,
don't run, politicians say but
too much scum is escaping
the reaper here, this fecal burg.
Too many car chases, hairy meth
bitches killing. Baldy gang bitches
killing. Cop bitches killing and
me scurrying from car to store
wishing I could redact "olly olly
oxen free" and quit hiding from
my fear of man, just tether my ass
like an ancient Cheyenne dog soldier
or better, bare my throat as a young,
weak wolf would but I can't do either—
why the hell should I?—too bad I can't
kill, just kill the bastards with words.
Line the murderers up and watch
them crumple on the lonely prairie.
Make them pray to any ancient God.
His low thunder after the distant fact
of lightning from a Sharps buffalo rifle.
God nasty, the cleansing lightning.
God explosive, the erotic rain of blood.

The Last of the Saiduka

> The Paiute Indians and the long-legged redheads did not
> get along well. The Indians accused these giants of being
> cannibals, and waged war against them. After a long
> struggle, a coalition of tribes trapped the remaining
> Saiduka in what is now called Lovelock Cave and set
> it aflame and the Saiduka were annihilated.
>
> Steve McNallen

And if you subscribe to legends
these *Saiduka* were all baked
dead with the exception of one
drooling *vata loca*, who looked
like a blend of Raggedy Ann
and the "Bride of Frankenstein"
when she banged on my brain—
door vast months ago. Sleep
staggered, nose bleeding from
the high ammonia of morning,
I should've answered the bell
except those winged monkeys
from the *Wizard of Oz*
were swarming over me
and one had his simian
pecker pressed against
my tired ass and I didn't
want to get pregnant
so I was fighting with all
my macho might. When
I finally broke free, I saw
her car leaving my driveway.
She tried to get me the next
day and I would've answered
but I recognized her number
on the caller ID and all I could
think of was the week before
when I drove her drunken body

home and she assumed I was hot
for her and did a staggering strip
tease, lowering her slacks past
her hips all the way down to
her red pubic hairs making
me freak and run to my car.
I could never bring myself to
touch pale flesh so hellishly
adorned with fiery, red hair.
Red hair on the skin indicates
red worms in the brain.
Insane in the membrane.

Yet a couple days after that
I almost fucking relented.
For a moment (old fool
that I am) I was going
to let my heart touch hers.
My fat heart is an old cow,
an affectionate Holstein . . .
huge slobbering tongue
and glowing moon-pie eyes.
My mottled heart galumphs
into occasional fragrant fields
of sweet spring grass, blind
to the red stringiness and
the red memory eternal
of its own native flesh.
Yes, my heart occasionally
forgets its own foolish age,
but when it licked her pale
heart it sobered quite quickly.

Once I saw a turkey buzzard
dead on the side of the road.
I don't know why I stopped
my car and stared it down, but
one of its filthy, gnarled claws
still firmly grasped a chunk
of death-stink, maggoty meat.

That vile, leathery claw is
what I tasted when I licked
her *Saiduka* heart. I was going
to let my dark spirit touch her
but in a rare, velvet moment
of blessed sanity my ancestor
spirits decided they did not
want my fat corpse just yet.
They didn't want me carted
up to a white, heavenly sky
and fumbled like God did to
the great red-skinned Satan.

Aimee Nezhukumatathil

Oriental

Oh this is the perfect ruby, O from the velvet can't you see. O my goodness, what big eyes you have, considering your mom is Filipina. O my goodness, how light you are, considering your father is Indian. O egg roll, O General Tsao's chicken I cannot eat with chopsticks, O how I love dim sum.

Reach out and wave to the land of the rising sun. Reset your clock backwards. Rejoice: you were admitted to a prestigious college and didn't accept it. Recall how your father left India with a pompadour and a Real thirst for all things American. Rejoice, you are the perfect opportunity for equality, and even on this island Resort, you have the longest legs.

Enrich your life with tea and almond cookies in glassine Envelopes, and even though you Envy all girls with blue eyes and the giant box of crayons (complete with built-in crayon sharpener), Entire rooms of men will soon be Enchanted by your lovely dark locks. Enrage math teachers who want to throw erasers at you. Engrave a curlicue on your best friend's palm when she smears Vaseline on the locker handle of the boy who called your father a scalper. *Wrong Indian, idiot*. Enchant the priest downstairs when you tell him you once saw a real crucifixion in the Philippines.

Tall. At 5'5", you are the Tallest woman in your family for five generations. Tall tales about chasing water buffalo down the street. Tall tales about a white peacock who will eat cashews out of your cupped hand. Tall tales about bad women stealing coconuts from your tiny grandmother and the cobras who stung their thieving feet. Tall tales of thin bangles and silver anklets hammered into snakey designs, tall tales of the family elephant who stole the bundle of sugarcane you were saving for dessert. Tall tales of the filthy restaurants with sour pineapples strung like lights and secret games of mah-jongg stay inside and never in the home because these men are betting men, but there is one white man—the man with arms outstretched and bloodied—who looks down at you and smiles.

High School Picture Retake Day

When an octopus becomes stressed, it chomps
its arms one by one until it becomes a floaty salad.

The line of students is understandably worried: this
is the last chance for redemption. Neil parts
and parts his hair with the petite plastic comb
the photographer slipped him when he signed

in. Susan reties the grosgrain bow in her braid.
Everything is quiet but for tiny songs

of tiny combs whistling through hair. Everything is black
save for the single camera lamp and smudgy backdrop
painted to look like the student hovers among
beige and blue clouds. And maybe they do—the ones

who got it right the first time—soaring above the earth's
troposphere, but still a bit below the stratosphere.
When the last bell rings, there they are: flying
proud, able to exchange wallet-sized pictures

with other pretty people right away. No waiting
for two more months when no one cares anymore.

No closed eyes, no sticks of hair sprung out
like arrows, no bra straps showing, no
sleepy eyes—just perfectly pressed shirts
and smiles slit to show rows of neat teeth.

Natasha Rocas

The Pillowbook of Natasha Roka

1. On a day you might prepare deviled eggs.

On a day you might prepare deviled eggs, with pickles and flecked with paprika, a woman throws her walker down the stairs like tumbleweed, descends step by single step, salvages it once at the bottom, and walks on, the sidewalk gnawing on the plastic tip of a seditious shoelace.

2. Elegant things.

Eating oatmeal with chopsticks. Trains asleep in the snow. Philodendrons in terracotta pots. Cameo brooches. Amber lamps. Russian dolls with eyes not quite the same size. A Nath—the nose ring of an Indian woman. Heavy doors. Byzantine churches with mean poker faces. Depression-era glass the color of virgin olive oil. Wine corks. Arched windows, bony and matte.

3. Unsuitable things.

Stickers from apricots left on a stainless steel sink. A little girl lifting up her skirt for bubble gum. Dirty knives. Rhetorical questions. Earwax on Q-tips left on a bathroom sink. Wine stained teeth. Hanging undergarments out to dry on a balcony. Cold ceramic tile floors. Chewing on cotton. Post-nasal drip. Naughty shoes. Cold teeth. Squirrels who steal peanut butter dipped spoons at Forsyth Park. Writing your mother, Maria Roka of Kalikratia, from America to tell her you married "a Donna." People who methodically separate their dinner, planning the order in which they will eat their basmati rice, curried black beans, and broccoli sprigs.

4. Greek folk remedies.

Sage for an upset stomach or mouth ulcer. Ouzo for a toothache. Rags soaked in vinegar for drawing out fever. Alcohol rubbed on your tummy for cramps. Chamomile for insomnia or sties. Rice and olive oil for diarrhea. Honey and lemon juice for a sore throat. Garlic cloves for colds or warts. Reading the sludge of Turkish coffee overturned onto a clean linen napkin for anxiety about the present or future.

5. Hateful things.

Forcing your left-handed son to write right. A puckered scowl from an old Greek man in polyester pants because your feet are on the plastic subway chair. Vegetarians who bury your leather shoes and belt under a pile of sodden leaves. To taunt him, a younger brother bites the T-shirt of his older brother.

6. Things one discusses over a cup of Earl Grey

Blooming onions. Oyster houses with red shutters, grimy planks, barnacles, and a rooster weathervane. Marinating on your chaise longue reading lessons on hoodoo by Zora Neal Hurston. Gypsies in red truck caravans who sell tables, chairs, and watermelons—they bellow *"karpuzia, trapezia, karekles."* The slot in penny loafers. Children who refuse to eat waffles that a fly has landed on. Jack-o-lanterns carved from peeled acorns, a paler burnt orange.

7. Indications one needs a new bookshelf.

When Anna Koljaiczek's four potato-colored skirts, all layered atop the other, harbor Karen Volkman's revenants. When Federico García Lorca finds he is buried in Samuel Beckett's elusive mound.

8. I do not suppose the inmates.

I do not suppose the inmates in Greek prisons make license plates. Perhaps, instead, they paint icons—the gold-leafed halo of St. Sophia or St. Ephrin or St. Paraskevi. They sell them to the little church on Metropoleo Avenue that survived the Balkan Wars. That church, canary and perspiring, wears cranberry lipstick kisses stained on each icon and carries the prayers people send with flames of singed beeswax candles.

9. *Things that give an unclean feeling.*

Brown stains on the lip of a teacup. Dripping apple butter jars. Gelled hair. Heaving opossums living underneath a bathtub. Shoes worn without socks. Fruit flies on a blender. Damp cotton fields. Brothels. Sticky pennies in a car's cup holder. The word *moist*. Bulbous noses. A mother's spit used to wipe smudge from her child's mouth. Coffee stained teeth. The smell of burnt nickels on fingertips left after thrifting for clothes.

10. *Things that give a clean feeling.*

Lemongrass. Canvas boat shoes. Coconuts. Pencil shavings. Incandescent lighting. The word *vestibule*. Mechanical pencils sold in a German stationery shop. Boats folded from newspaper floating in a bowl of water. Wooden wedding spoons. Ripped seams of sugar snap peas. Aloe plants. Matches on the back of a toilet.

11. *Poetic subjects.*

Expecting your brother to hit you for having thrown all the chess pieces on the floor; rather he licks your arm and blows on it—his air feels like wet pottery. Middle-aged men who tuck in sweatshirts. Children who time how long they brush their teeth. Knowing who is descending the stairs by the sound of a person's footsteps. The brötchen lady who rides a red bike, nicked and rowdy, and howls into the stairwells with a shrill voice only a ninety-nine year old German woman might have, at seven in the morning. The red and gold pendant you would speak into when no one sat with you at lunch during the first grade. People unapologetic for their vesicant garlic breath. The patch of gray hair your grandmother misses when she dyes her hair by herself. Men who serve twenty-two years in the military and still drop rifles while at the range.

12. *Things one wants to throw away in a fancy red trash can.*

Moms who bring celery, peanut butter, and raisins (ants on a log) for afternoon snack time. Un-valentines tinged with slightly scorched, knotted bread cookies. Boys who lure girls into bushes with pearls.

13. *Sayings a southern grandpa might use.*

I says. Son of a biscuit eater. You haven't written a poem *in a month of Sundays. I ran over hell's half acre.* We're having colcannon for *supper.* Where is my *billfold?* Your cousin was *drunker than a coot. He's done got too big for his britches.* She was *happier than an anteater on a picnic. Lawdy, lawdy, lawdy.*

14. *After spending two months in Greece.*

After spending two months in Greece, you tell your Giagia (grand-mother), *I am going to take you home with me, put you in my jean pocket* (and you would because you drink Turkish coffee with her in demitasse cups and accept the thimble or coin purse she might give you because you like tiny whatnots). Giagia, weeping eggplant in salt, replies, ". . . *and from this day forward, I will not eat so that I may fit.*"

15. *Things one does not like to do.*

Praying before dinner, touching the hinges of your shoulders as you make a cross, or taking communion because you can't tell your Giagia you are Greek, but not Greek Orthodox. In fact, God is a husk, and you cannot bear the idea of sharing that silver spoon with an entire church of beehived biddies.

16. *Banes of my existence.*

Conversations that are broken tiled and gray. Thirty-nine cent stamps. Lentils dried on a soup bowl. Roof rats that open everything in a pantry to find they like nothing you eat. Wilted salad. Garlic presses. Putting a duvet on a comforter with no one's help. Plastic cutlery.

17. *Things that give one a feeling of accomplishment.*

Making tiropitas with your Giagia, pressing the edges of the folded cheese pies with forks as if holding a sparrow and using his feet to stamp the leavened dough. The night you leave your soul in a paper bag in Lit-tle Five Points, Atlanta. Pretending to receive an order at a local health food grocer you work for when you are actually reading *The Hound of Baskervilles* by Sir Arthur Conan Doyle; you harbor Sherlock Holmes and the hound under a stack of invoices when you hear a coworker dragging his mired feet along the linoleum. Weeding out the beds of a garden.

18. In Loutsa, you have neither washboard nor washing machine.

In Loutsa, you have neither washboard nor washing machine. You slosh around in a red bucket to wash your clothes. You become a villager preparing for the grape harvest, but rather than grapes, you are stomping socks or a plum voile sundress—your feet stained with squid ink.

19. Squalid Things.

Herman Melville's negation. Biting the skin around one's fingernails. A baby born sucking her thumb. The word *squelched*. A bearded man with ringworms skulking below his jawbone. Spit that collects into white mounds on the corners of mouths.

20. There can only be so many times.

There can only be so many times one may slam the refrigerator door before the apple cider vinegar falls from atop—and one will note that day because from that moment onward, they will no longer spend the same amount of time deciding what to eat for dinner as they do selecting a pair of underwear.

21. Pleasant things.

Calendula colored rocking chairs, sturdy and spotted like the legs of an Irish woman. Sun porches that house a bonsai tree transplanted from a brick—call her Mortimer. She is an anarchist and would survive a red tide. A homeless man named Brown who makes roses from palm leaves and asks only for aspirin in return because he has a headache and Ashmore's has no work for him. The mother (unfiltered pith) of apple cider vinegar. Sitting on a sidewalk in May, eating vanilla ice cream and tangelos while listening to Otis Redding. Red gingham aprons. Volksmarches. The tiny *t*'s, protective blessings, your grandmother crosses when planes pass overhead.

22. Disheartening Things.

When your mother has epilepsy and bedsores and a bad case of the—*rusty and off-key harmonica wails*—slumpish sloth blues. When one returns from vacation to find her car has a flat tire. When one makes a red cabbage salad, reaches for the pepper grinder, and finds it has just set free a colony of peppercorns on your lunch.

23. *I rode in a Lancia, foul mouthed and shedding.*

I rode in a Lancia, foul mouthed and shedding, into the mountains of the Peloponnesus with a boy, bearded and knock-kneed, the one who once asked if he could "kiss me properly," to see his family's house that was suffering from emphysema. The villagers ordered her to be torn down soon because she was two-hundred, forlorn, and her cough was awaking the neighbors. He tells me he will rebuild the house one day; he'll mend the cracks and suture the roof's stitches.

24. *Things one remembers about childhood (from ginger snaps to Rothenberg).*

Ginger snaps and *moustokoulouria* (grape must cookies). Blues mix-tapes your father made for you, muddy watered and unfaithful. Little diamond windows cut into mustard seeded doors. The toothpicks school nurses used for monthly lice checks. At age seven, "giving birth" to a pumpkin baby, auburn haired and partial to tapioca pudding, that you carried on your bony hip. Your older brother reading vampire stories upside down on the living room couch, rubbing his head against the carpet, and your mother telling him he shouldn't because he'll lose his hair. The red plaid skirt you wore with hot pink leggings. (Latch) keys. A father, after his family has arrived in a cobblestoned Rothenberg, taking his children home because they forgot to brush their teeth.

25. *Things one remembers about childhood (from smashed sandwiches to underwear).*

The way your best friend smashed parts of a ham and cheese sandwich before eating it (a task almost impossible to achieve with a peanut butter and jelly). The girl who asked you how to say "god" when you gave Greek lessons to your second grade class on Tuesday afternoons; rather than telling her you didn't know, you created a word, wrote a libel against him. *There's a Hippopotamus Under My Bed,* or perhaps *Amelia Bedelia.* Footie pajamas you received via mail-order after saving Smucker's jelly UPC labels. Making a shoebox diorama of Anne Frank's secret annex from the same paisley contact paper your mother cut into hearts to decorate her bathroom walls. Pleated khakis. The ochre and kidney-shaped vomit vessels that lurked in a school nurse's office. Using a shell as a Barbie clothing hamper. The red M&Ms your second grade teacher, Mrs. Miller, did not like. Your parents giving you a package of underwear on your older brother's birthday because you did not understand the concept of birthday gift giving.

26. *Things that make one's heart beat faster.*

Sledding down grass hills on a cardboard box you wear like an afghan. Listening to pecans fall upon your roof as the trees yawn. Smashing pennies on railroad tracks. Blood oranges.

27. *Adorable things.*

Your mom belting out *"stretch armstrong nickelodeon shoes"* on election day '88 after making you red, white, and blue pancakes for breakfast. Homeless men who when asking if they may pick a few of the pecans in your yard, really mean a trash bag full. Platonic crushes. Greek inscriptions your father writes you on a torn paper bag, despite his knowing you cannot read Greek; you do, however, make out the words *"have"* and *"garlic."* Montana men who wear argyle socks and cure old trestle tables. Your best friend's pillow case collection. Asking to take your grandmother's picture—she refuses, instead giving you an old passport photo, nineteen-fiftied and stamped like a branded billy goat, because that's how she wants you to remember her. Improvising Prince's *Raspberry Beret* while porchin' it on a ledge with boys named Slim, Nor, and Marc.

28. *Three weeks after you've told your Giagia you are a vegetarian.*

Three weeks after you've told your Giagia you are a vegetarian, she wakes you to ask *why* you no longer eat sardines or chicken or lamb. It's one of those mornings where she might have forced warm milk upon you were you nine again. She tells you *"Tous indianos (the Indians) are vegetarian and you are Greek."* And because it is Wednesday, you tell her you are in fact Indian and not Greek—and what's more, you run an underground cocaine ring in the flat basement.

29. *An apology to the boy.*

An apology to the boy whose copy of *Archie and Mehitabel* I borrowed: I didn't mean to get mandarin juice on pages 17-24, but I didn't have a place to put the peel and your book seemed far less intimidating than my aunt's maudlin table.

30. *Rare things.*

A fruit stand on the side of the road that sells peaches and perch. Your older brother constructing a creature from a blank envelope found on your car floor—he calls him mow-mow, a duck who speaks like a toothless old man who has lost the plastic and sea-foam green half-moon meant to store his dentures. Sei Shonogon. Leaving your jeans to soak on a scorching tiled balcony in Greece to find them boiling three hours later. Billie Holiday's *Strange Fruit.*

Martha Silano

I Wanted to Be Hip

but with a kid strapped in the stroller
my size 38EE breasts my husband

accidentally *hi there mammary glands*
but with not knowing which belt

black with silver studs or multi-colored sash
which sandals wedge or flip-flop

then which flip-flop beaded or cushioned
instead I got escorted to the elevator for the un-hip

child on each hip for the totally un-tuned-in
though all of us wanted to emanate

lavender cowboy boots a sparkly amber shawl
so we might gesticulate with flair

wanted let's face it the whole world to wobble
when we watoozied into a room

chins jutting never tucked under
like a sleeping gull more like mama killdeer

feigning a broken wing
Remember the first hip huggers?

I thought it was 1968
but my US Navy father dug in his closet

to 1944 found the sailor suit
complete with low-rise bell bottoms almost

killed him he couldn't button up

This Parenting Thing

which I love which I hate
the love part easy not torture at all

like his asking *spell furniture* while we wait
outside the Rogue River Fly Shop

like checking to see if the faeries came
his digging with a blue shovel while I weed

the broccoli the kale and even asking
over and over for a gummy worm

which I will not give him he's already
had three and that's just the beginning

the first few words of the brook
that flashes and foams that keeps on

with its garter-snake awe with its ant fascination
all of it not yet drooped not yet fallen in a heap

till all that's left's a rose hip
a hip you could dry and make a tea with

but will you? But that's the least of it
barfing croup a temperature of 105

the day he rolled off the changing table
the day he ate the insect repellant *just be lucky*

they're healthy how dare you hate his sneakiness
his thrown-out crusts just be lucky you don't live

in Nigeria where polio's making a comeback
just be glad you don't live nearly anywhere else

but what about my one-year old her three or four
or sometimes fifteen nighttime feedings

can I hate what sleeplessness does to a brain
like I'm caught in amber whenever

multicellular beings formed
dragging along reaching for sugar caffeine

like some brachiopod some primitive bivalve
a little closer I'll admit to all that lives

but not quite sane when she starts to choke
on a piece of grocery list the firemen storming

where is she? to de-lodge the marble or dime
to turn her upside down and whack her

till the bead or pebble slips out
though by the time they arrive

I've pulled out the guilty party and she's cooing
Love it? Love it? Yep yep especially

the notes that come from school
Riley helped a sad friend today

or looking up to see in place of her face
a lime green plastic plate anticipating

my *peek-a-boo!* though could live without
the half-way through yoga right when we're about

to start on shoulder stands *I think she wants
her mama* though bet you'd find it hard to believe

feeding her mashed peas and rice I'm already
longing for the silver and turquoise spoon

for what falls to her sleeve but then she's screaming
and I'm screaming over her screaming

carrying on the conversation hating
what she takes longing for evening's relief

though longing too for morning though dreading the bib
and the apple sauce wriggling her into pink plush jeans

though not wanting her anywhere close
to asking for keys and meanwhile my son

can't stop asking where is it who has it
and all about the kid who owns it now

forever and ever until he discovers there's one with spots
and that one will do which lasts about fifteen minutes

my whole life snatched away for procurement forms
for reading him *Goodnight Moon* and *Click, Clack Moo*

for lifting her up to the doctor's scale
watching the numbers line up

John Rybicki

The Moon, the Moon—She's You

Keep your moonshine in an alfalfa field for me to haul around with one finger in the bottle. Your moonshine in a bottle. Your moonshine at a jobsite to paint the clapboard houses—I'll make one stripe along your nose. The littler brushes we'll dip to paint moon-wet lipstick on the sleepers, extra hearts on the sides of horses. I'll climb your shoulders, then you'll climb mine. Our war paint on the barn we'll smear with lune hearts that burn holes through wood. We're straw. Our tongues tangle into ropes we're so frightened the earth might inhale and tug us apart. Say my tongue slips to paint a kiss along the silky underbelly behind the knee. It would hurt your eyes to look at us: we're kissing burn marks, a scorching border around our land until a wall of shining moon seals us in. I drift to snow when the work is done, drift with a pail tossing moon slop to our skeletons, then turn back and there's that light like comfort falling fleshy from your window. You paint with the ache God gave us, your blood light on the snow from where you lift your nightgown and peel back one rib near the window. Out you pour that which guides me back and I rub a little on my face, cough the nails up that nail down my bones. We're rosy now under the covers, your moon slipping past so swiftly now. You say there's only one day like ours, and I fold your rib down, a little moth of light sparking at the ends of my fingers.

Steve Scafidi

After a Photo of the Author in a National Magazine

The scuzzy one smoking outside the Gas-N-Go
        who really wants to know your name
and get up in your face a little. Down on his luck
    hucklebuck with the face of a knife.

How did it happen? You win a poetry prize
        and after work a friend takes your picture
and all is well until you see the magazine—
    this stranger I am shines like a pearl.

This creepy little guy squinting at the world.
        His over-sized white foam ball cap
casts a shadow over his black piggy eyes.
    Cousin to a fly and dumb as a mitten.

But worst of all is the smile crooked and hidden
        in the beard like a smirk on a worm
before it bites. Here is the devil's assistant.
    His good idea persistent as molasses—

he pokes the body with a pitchfork as it passes.
        Here is the guarded laugh of
satisfaction doing the lord's simple work.
    Sidekick to a jerk. Smiles when you fall.

Oh mother I am sorry. It is not your fault
        that I have grown petty and difficult
and small, the perfect example of an asshole.
    Who hassles cashiers. Who has no patience.

The kind of person who cusses at every occasion
        for the joy of it and who holds a grudge
like a magic dollar to his chest and drinks—
    who thinks even this poem will win a prize

—and drives and assumes everyday he will die
        in prison and deserve it and so wakes
each morning and kisses his family goodbye as if
    this is it. Somebody should get him a Tic-Tac.

Today all of the comely and earnest sad sacks
        of the country who like to fancy
themselves poets and writers can see it's true.
    Someone made a mistake. They must be joking.

This man is full of self regard and of loathing
        and looks it. He looks like
he might kill you in your sleep. Oh, he looks
    like what we fear—standing at the door.

He looks like a million bucks in that cap and I am
        sure the sun is in his eyes is why
he smiles like that. Something chews its leg off
    and limps from the trap. Here is beauty

in agony says the fox. "What he said," says the rat.
        I drag my potbelly along the tracks
of the day and it is all right. It is only a picture.
    Mother, please—throw it in the trash.

David Clewell

The Perfect Stranger

> He saved my baby's life, then just walked away. He was a
> perfect stranger. He still is.
>
> At the scene of the fire
>
> For Patricia, eventually

No one knows how he makes his way in this imperfect world.
He doesn't have a come-on, a gimmick, or a pitch—
to say nothing of a proper name he'll own up to.
He's so good at whatever he does, it calls for no introduction.
His face is a composite of every low profile he's kept.
No perfect likeness will ever be sold as a bobblehead figurine.
He has no identifying marks. He'll never be caught dead
standing out in a crowd. If he sits down next to you at the bar,
the last thing on his mind is where have you been all his life.
He can't be out looking for that kind of trouble.
But should he come across the purse you left behind in a hurry,
you'll find it at the door in the morning, everything inside
perfectly intact, without a note of explanation. It's already more
than he really wanted to know: who you are and where you live.

By now he's in a rush of his own, all but disappearing
into one more day's white noise. But he'll be there
under a third-story window when the smoke starts pouring out
and a mother drops her baby down as softly as she can pray.
By noon he'll be at the courthouse, posting bail after unlikely bail.
His afternoon's a quintessential walk in the park—
he'll have some CPR to give. A Professor-of-Humanities Chair to
    endow
at a school that's gone MBA-crazy. Maybe he'd say it's nothing,

really, if only he felt like talking. What else does he have to do
except to show up where he's so completely unexpected?
It's never going to be his day to drive the office carpool.
He won't be counted on, looked forward to.
                                        Statistically speaking,
we're usually strangers ourselves, and I don't know how in the world
some days most of us are nothing if not civil to each other.
But the perfect stranger would seem to be another matter entirely.

Sometimes in his sleep he dreams up secret imperfections:
he's washing whites with colors. Forgets to turn off the lights.
Or there's a knife stuck deep in the toaster again,
mud on the dress boots or blood in the sink,
the wrong-size spoon stirring quietly in the soup.
His bid for a perfect game is spoiled by a 3-2 pitch in the dirt.
But who's he kidding? When he wakes up, there's not a chance
in hell those things will happen.
                                When I woke up today I thought
of him sitting down for breakfast, bending over a plate of eggs
cooked, of course, to perfection. And I was strangely relieved
to think he might be out there somewhere, carrying the ball
for everyone who can't quite measure up. But then again
he doesn't have the likes of you to lie down next to,
his concentration so utterly blown on a regular basis.

Surely you must know by now how often you're the reason
for these imperfect words—even when it doesn't seem that way
at first. But notice how, just four lines up, a perfect stranger
led me back to you. And he'll be out of here soon enough.
This poem actually began so long ago, it's not even funny.
Before the perfect stranger came to me, I was working hard
on the Moon, sweating out some Space-Race-paranoia epic, or so
I supposed. But even on the Moon I couldn't stop myself from saying
sometimes it's hard to tell apart the two extremes of love—
the giddy weightlessness, the stubborn sense of gravity. And then I said
we're better off not trying.

                    Back down here on Earth
you and I get it mostly right in the long bed of our life together,
some days especially beautiful for the flaws that show up there:
how you make off to the other side with the blankets in your sleep.
How I often talk in mine, resorting to the future-perfect tense—
maybe tomorrow, next week, or more surprising years from now,
I *will have learned*, finally, to believe it when you tell me
I'm the only less-than-perfect one for you. That much still
could happen. But I promise that's another poem completely.

And whenever I wake up that absolutely uncovered,
there's no way to pretend that we don't see
you're about to get what you've had coming all along.
That would be me, so excited that somehow I'm still flying
the flag you were raising over and over in my dream.
And I've got the whole day to explain, if I have to. Nowhere else
I'm unexpected. I already know by heart exactly who you are
and where you live and how we're about to fit together
pretty damn well, if not perfectly, again.

Cathleen Calbert

Pirating

I was a boy before I became a woman. My father hid his bastard
daughter in the guise of a sister's son. I skipped rocks far across

the water my steps longer than any girl's. As soon as I slipped
on a dress I met a boy who belonged to the sea who wasn't

"worth a groat" so said my father. He would give us nothing
from his rows of tobacco. I left the plantation in flames prepared

for the life of a seawife honest if rough. I was to sew up holes
in the lads' jackets knot the line and wash down the deck. Except

we were boarded by self proclaimed kings of the sea and given
our choice keelhauling or putting in with them. While my man

mended sail the captain all in calico hiked up my skirt his hand
over my mouth. Would I have called out? As my father took his

wife's maid so Captain Jack took me. One cannot call that
seduction but once done there was a kind of love as harsh as the sun.

Our lives were not easy scurvy the bloody flux and the
men like as not to shoot themselves or blow us up drunk on rum

that ran as freely as ditch-water. When we could we plundered
brigantines laden with sugar bound for Madagascar and Mozambique.

We helped ourselves to citrons tamarinds black bananas honey
and coconuts matelote and mangoes sweeter than perfume.

On islands smaller than my father's farm I went turtling (the flesh
made a fine stew) and I picked up a spider monkey which I wore

on one shoulder like a lady's lopsided wig. I saw the southern lights
seabirds as big as angels and as fierce. In Jamaica Jack bought

fair winds from a wind-seller. He tried to buy me outright
from Mr. Bonny but the magistrate said that I should be in chains

for turning libertine so we married ourselves by starlight then rode
the currents countryless. "Where do you hail from, brothers?"

sailors cried. "From the sea!" we yelled as if self-sprung like Venus
in her shell or Athena. I fought as a man far easier to load powder

or stuff a cutlass in breeches and a tar's blouson but the crew knew
me to be a woman as well. I was to foretell all storms and keep

devilfish from bleeding their toes or serpents from coiling themselves
around the anchor. Oh those boys were a superstitious lot jellies

seemed sunken virgins to them and giant polyps bore the faces of
lost mothers. Scylla himself lifted his six mouths into the spray

and called them to a watery grave. When I bled they begged me
to lie unclothed under the night sky so the currents would follow

my bent and my body would frighten the behemoths that breathed
whirlwinds. I indulged them more seawitch than seaman then.

Yet when we were attacked I demanded that each hand fight
like a man or die like a dog. "Join or drown," we told the crew

of a schooner among them a pretty boy his face as smooth as a
girl's. I took him below and loosened my clothes to show

I was not what I seemed my chest as smooth as his cheeks.
He undressed and disclosed breasts larger than my own.

Sister to sister we lay together. But above deck we gave no quarter
the last two left standing under the black flag. "A hell of our making,"

declared the judge. "Hang the dogs. Have mercy on their souls."
All swung. Captain Jack they strung up on the bluffs of Kingston.

Mary and I pled our bellies. The seeds of men had taken root.
No steps and string for us until we were relieved of our burdens.

I held my girl in the damp gaol cell. I felt her heat rise to the skies
rise to heaven. Alone then I obliged the world with an orphan.

But someone my father? intervened enough bullion and I was free
to leave with a bastard of my own to raise. I tell you the old man

can set a place for me and mine all the days of his life if he likes.
I still walk on water. My daughter makes a fine first mate.

Together we have rounded Cape Horn the Cape of Good
Hope and gone on to uncharted waters where live the famed

fish tailed maids whose hair is as green as seafire. After sunset
their skin looks like the skin of dead men their eyes unholy emeralds.

Even I count them unlucky then but at dawn they bathe on
rocks and comb their seaweed tresses as they gaze into mirrors

encrusted with starfish and abalone at a past of endless waves
living in a way backwards as is their wont since they worship

the moon not the sun. They shall summon two sailors neither men
nor women to a feast under the sea whenever we tire of roving.

Caroline Knox

Text Panel

#78 a & b. While the subject of #38—Mrs. *Fafnir Blenkinsop* (1942?)—
in which the gloves seem to be a food of straw, linsey-woolsey (poke-
weed dye), and mustard seed, is seated at the spinet in a pose
traditionally connected with St. Cecilia (as Anguissola), still #14 shows
Dr. Blenkinsop reading to his bride from the Elder Edda, with their
daughter (Postlethwaite?) on the left, an installation. "Of course, of
course," Mrs. B. bursts out. "I always wondered why *Little House on the
Prairie* sounded so much like Hemingway. Rose Wilder Lane went and
redacted the story, and that's why! She and Hemingway were journal-
ists!" Where were we? #78 a & b. Fetch the waybread from your moose-
foot wall pocket. O *esca viatorum!* Adorn your temple with the
speech-belt for a slide tour, a tour slide of the contact zone event. The
speech-belt seems to be a food of snow.

Roy Jacobstein

Nibbles

Where are all the sober men in black suits
    & bowlers, their umbrellas' handles curled
        properly over their left forearms, pointing

inward? Where is that biker angry
    he was forced to swerve when I stepped
        from the kerb into his acceleration, rasped

Watch it, bahstahd trailing
    his leather epaulettes like a knotted rope.
        Where the old buildings, the rubble still

palpable three decades post-Blitz? Where
    the tuppence, thruppence, hā'-p'ny, bob?
        Everything's so new to one whose notion

of London was fired and fixed
    by Jonson & Johnson, Eliot & Blake
        (*the mind-forg'd manacles, the yellow smoke*)

& confirmed in the austere yet chic
    company of a quasi-radical Parisienne.
        Quels beaux yeux! she cooed as she elided

her ivory fingertips across my virginal eyelids.
    Where are you *ce matin*, Chantal? It's all changed,
        the eyes belong to the models now, their gaze

pierces with the *hauteur* that must be *Leçon Une*
 in Runway Comportment. The mannequins too,
  with nipples the size of the Hope Diamond. *Nibbles*

my nephew says, indicating his desire
 to nurse. Amidst quickening commerce,
  a beauty with beaded hair approaches,

asking directions. *I'm just in from Addis*
 I say, for she must be Ethiopian: that thin,
  straight, regal nose, so valued in the West.

But she's skeptical—such felicitous
 coincidence. Should I prove it, unfurl
  my wallet, show her the twenty-birr note

with her late last Emperor, Haile Selassie,
 on its face? (Proud Lion of Judah, *Ras Tafari*,
  Jamaica's Living God.) Alas, the hotel map

I extract instead from my pen-pocked
 breast pocket's limited to Goodge Street,
  hence inutile. We part in Amharic, *goodbye*

the only word of her ancient tongue
 I could master, *goodbye*, & onward she flutters
  through this land where she'll always stand out,

in that way non-sooted moths briefly lit
 the Industrial Revolution's oaks. More store-
  fronts on this street that pulses the bounty

of 21st Century free trade: New Look, Gap
 Kids, United Colors of Benetton. I can take it
  no longer, turn down a side road, past a mobile

phone store, its glut of choices
 clotting the window, past the Hare
  Krishna Centre, into a small park

where tranquil in the distance stands
    the classic red telephone booth from which
        Clark Kent (né Jor-El) would have emerged

transformed, had a Brit not a poor immigrant
    in New York created Superman (& Kryptonite).
        Abruptly the spring sun has riven the usual horde

of leaden clouds, inducing a squint
    & an illusion of warmth. The masses
        you loved yet scorned have gathered

at my feet, the same useless purple iridescence
    flecking their neck feathers, & they still linger,
        even after it's clear one has no seed to scatter.

The Unknown Albeit, or
While Reading a Friend's
Prize-Winning Book on Love's
Vicissitudes He Writes about Words

For Robert Thomas

Rhachis, dumka, grisette, iku, kolache, azagur—
    you're doing it again, amigo, sending me
        to meaning, avid as ever. So I enter *aa*

at www.Dictionary.com, find neither
    anti-aircraft nor Associate in Arts, but lava
        having a rough surface, though transmuted

in your hands to something *glorious, black-*
    faceted, trillion-spined. Rolling, I enter *trillion,*
        imagining hothouse blooms, forgetting

those 12 zeroes trailing the lonely one.
    Well, who wouldn't be confused by now,
        being confronted by the unknown albeit

mellifluous *mokihana*, lovely double spondee
    you've wed to Mt. *Waialeale*, a site looming
        above a leper colony in Tonga or Vanuatu

or Fiji, no doubt, but leading me to desire
    a dish of *wahine* . . . or is it *haole*? Never mind,
        here comes *szatmari*, your next seductress,

flashing skirts, black boots, scarlet lace,
    some ecstatic dance that sizzles and burns,
        I surmise, for your book's fiery and on *love,*

its tang and its char, the one subject I learned
    to shun like it's the electric prod, I'm the bum
        steer—but even the e-reference is stumped,

though clueless it's not, proffering
　　alternatives, crypto-homonymous kin. Thus
　　　　I'm queried do I intend *Satu Mare*, and lo!,

only a click away arises a medieval walled city
　　in Transylvania, setting for Stoker's gothic horror
　　　　novel whose vampire lends his name to a bevy

of diminutive tropical plants (genus *Draculae*)
　　having bizarre, sinister-looking purple flowers
　　　　with pendulous scapes and hyper-motile lips—

which sounds a hell of a lot like the love
　　I would write about if I wrote about love,
　　　　which is why I don't, but it's sure good

to know when I reject *Satu Mare*
　　there's still *stammerer* and *stud mare*
　　　　left for me to consider, and I do.

Nin Andrews

Depression

Look, I've Been Cut in Half!
One side has eyes. The other is blind.
One has a heart, the other a knife.
There is so much distance between my halves,
you could drive a car right through me.
Maybe you think it's simple:
on one side there's shadows and the other light.
On one side there's dreams and the other life.
But yesterday I saw a cab run over a cyclist.
When I looked up, a crow was circling.
The sun turned black. No one knew my name,
not even me. *What do you want?* God asked.
Everything, I said. But it wasn't true.
In the distance between what one says
and the other means, there's so much ache.
Sometimes I can't help it.
I talk to myself. *Let's go*, I always say.
Let's get out of this fucking place.
Then she wraps herself around me like a wave.

Dear Professor

Dear Professor,

I had a hard time on the second part
of the exam. I was tired.
I think I studied too hard.
I kept stopping to think,
and I had to go to the bathroom,
but I was afraid to go
because I thought you might think
I was cheating in there.

Dear Professor,

You gave that problem
about driving down the freeway at 60 MPH
in a VW bug and hitting a truck
that was driving at 75 MPH,
and you wanted to know happened next,
and I figured the answer was
to drive a truck from now on.

Dear Professor,

When I was in your office
and you showed me that problem
about the weight lifter and the dumb bells,
I kept smiling and saying yes,
but I didn't really understand it.
I tried, but it's like we were speaking
different languages. I think
new professors do that.
They get lost in translation.
So I thought maybe I should tell you
that when a student smiles and says yes
she usually means she has no idea
what you're talking about.

Danielle Pafunda

Who Chose Marie Antoinette

I was a college girl, and I'd been brow down
on the quad. Earlier, I'd been stringing along
in a third floor room, silhouette vice grip
on the stroll below.

I knew, for instance, the gun was loaded.
A long rope, the hiss of pipe, the fat
valise.

So, you might say I was recruited.
I left that world in my cotton duck.
I didn't pack his monogrammed fiber
or her wheeze of pearls. Don't think
we didn't know what we were about.

We raked every road sign with a Molotov.

Who Chose Golda Meir

They taught me to curry favor, as one would
curry the horse, fat ribbons in my sleek. Well.
I hid from them the spoons we were. To each
other in seizure. Her there. The white shag.

They cauterized the wound in the safe, the bonds
stymied. But it was too late. I was already,
with my knapsack, *en route*. One would have
thought more relish.

But then, hadn't I? Right under their fine
cartilage, hadn't my one lone vessel slipped
the latch and wrestled lengthwise
on the flagstone in the drive? It was a gore.

Agape with its ventricles, pleasured to end.

Joseph Millar

Harriet Matthias Wickersham

They put me in charge of the big house
after the strokes finally took you,
left me alone in your sumptuous apartment
marking time till the final sale closed, watching
re-runs of *The Untouchables*, smoking Panama Red.
The grand furniture skulked in the corners
fuming with resin and camphor:
the mahogany armoire, the ringed chest of drawers
stout relatives I'd met once as a child
carried away piece by piece
to their split-level in Cherry Hill.
My mother's portrait gleamed there, bright ghost
presiding over the wine-colored rug
where dense ethers rose from the garden,
drifted against the windows.

I moved my friends in: their saxophones,
their tapes of Bo Diddley and Howlin' Wolf.
Mr. Adler practiced Chopin upstairs
on a scarred baby grand. I collected
the rents. When the hot water
thermostat failed to shut off
steam rose from the basins and toilets
till the supply pipe blew free of the heater
filling the basement with sludge.
Water surrounded us all that year:
the morning I thought I'd seen your face
in the lilac tree under the fire escape
I emptied your ashes into Westtown Lake
where my mother's had floated so long before.

I harried my pinched, narrow poems, failed
imitations of Tu Fu and James Wright.
Weekends I soaked through a languorous narcissism
in the opulent, claw-footed tub
under clouds of vapor, touching myself.
All I had was my body
which kept waking me up to eat, to shit,
to labor, hungover, for a local builder
at a piss-elegant site called the Joie de Vivre,
fake mansions perched on a hillside
tricked out with gables and vaulted ceilings
in a sparse woods beside the Expressway.
I wore a red sweatshirt in winter,
burned trash in the bonfire, stacked scaffolding,
swung a pick into the frozen mud.

The night your lawyers signed salvage contracts
I stole the leaded smoke-blue windows,
the oak front door and its iron hasp,
tore out the off-white Williamsburg fireplace
while a fat moon lit the front porch like a pond
and a cold wind rattled the glistening bandage
of six-mill stapled plastic. I stashed
the goods in a storage locker,
thinking of my future fantasy home, then
never went back to claim them.

Grandmother, fragile, querulous solitary,
no one could stand you for long.
Your husband whose name you forbade us to speak
left you the same year my mother was born,
driven out by your fits of pique.
And I was surely no prize myself
in my watch cap and worn Levi's
restless for California,
bored with stories of my mother's youth.

Lord knows I've never wished you'd come back
though maybe you have, in another body
as your hero HP Blavatsky suggests,
one that's forgotten the quiet evenings
we enjoyed in front of your television,
Tuesday nights watching *Gunsmoke*
that rainy autumn I slept on the third floor—
you drinking mint tea in the high bed
you rarely left, a satin scarf
wrapped around your aquiline head,
and I in the gold chair, wrecked on hashish,
while fall storms blew through the sycamores
and the stern marshal kept order in Dodge.

Dick Allen

The Waterfall Collector

"What you collect," he said, "tells more about you
than what you avoid. I, for instance,
avoid shutting doors of all kinds, especially cabinet doors,
and I dislike the kind of people whose conversation
consists mainly of barley soup. I don't like barley soup,
nor the dullness of mid-Ohio, mid-Indiana, mid-Illinois,
since driving across them seems like brushing your teeth.
But these are just quirks. What I collect are waterfalls,
high waterfalls, like those of the Columbia River Gorge:
Bridal Veil, Coopery, Elowah, Horsetail, Multnomah.
Yet also the cute little waterfalls without names
that only drop ten or fifteen feet or so into pine forests."

Alongside us, dressed in a tourist's plaid shirt,
he was leaning against a railing facing Buttermilk Falls,
a medium-sized waterfall of upper New York State,
his shirtsleeves rolled up, camera case at his side. We were just gazing
as one does at waterfalls, looking steadily
at all that force and rush, some part of our minds or souls
knowing there had to be an answer there
and not just white noise. "I've got pictures," he told us,
"of every important waterfall in America,
and not only that. I've got a whole room, you know,
of waterfall-related things: souvenir dishtowels
with waterfalls painted on them in lots of colors,
rocks I took from pools and rivers under waterfalls,
View-Master slides, waterfall key rings, waterfall coffee mugs,
waterfall suspenders,
a Yankee Candle that smells like a waterfall in Brunswick, Maine,

waterfall taffy, waterfall fudge, and my favorite:
a wind-up waterfall music box, seven inches high,
where the water's made of silver-painted tin from post-war Japan,
and it plays that Marlene Dietrich song, 'Falling in Love Again.'"

We listened, as one does to strangers you're stuck in line with,
who don't take themselves too seriously, are just trying to make small
    talk
and yet terribly need to let you know they're not just anyone,
that desire for importance, uniqueness,
stronger, I suspect, than the need for love. *I'm someone, someone,*
    someone.
I won't just die.
And I was half-thinking of my father, a collector, too: covered bridges,
our whole house filled with covered bridges memorabilia,
bridges over troubled waters, that sort of thing,
so I felt I understood. "There's something about waterfalls
that just gets me," the collector said out of the corner of his mouth,
"gets me right here." And I swear he thumped his chest, his voice
    choked up
before he walked away with a "See ya,"
which of course he almost certainly never would again,
fulfilling his quest, following rivers and streams
right to their fall lines where the harder rocks
descend to the softer rocks. Once again,
I remembered how many times I'd vowed to start collecting
stamps, postcards, *Star Trek* figures, Weebles because I love the slogan,
"*Weebles wobble but they can't fall down,*"
and the pun of "*Yea, though I walk through the Valley of the Shadow of*
    Death
I shall fear no weeble" and from *The Shadow:*
"*Who knows what weeble lurks in the heart of man?*"
. . . How glorious, I tell myself,
to collect something, to have your world all lined up on shelves
or in small containers at your feet! How in control that must feel,
like being President and forming a coalition
or the wife of a President and owning so many thousands of shoes
even Nancy Sinatra would be frightened. How wonderful
to gaze at your collection and think *mine, all mine,*
rubbing your hands together,

or to show it off for hours, or to insure it. That, I thought,
must be what's wrong with me—no collections,
nothing but odds and ends and here and there's.
Randomness. Whim. Chaos. Fragments. Zen. No wonder
I think of my life as brushstrokes in the snow,
a falling into space. No wonder
my life seems so unreal. . . . The waterfall
loomed high above us and kept coming down. In the tiny shop next
    door,
the clerks wore earplugs. Each clerk looked involved, entrusted,
counting change, taking credit cards, anonymous, unmemorable,
just working along, *can't help it*, making the days go by.

Amy Gerstler

Mid-Life Lullaby

Fear not the tarnish and diminishments of age
or its insane revelations as you creak, leak and freak
your way to the grave. Never relinquish ties
to exiles, to juiced-up boozers and the bamboozled.
Like you, they're solid citizens anguish nearly polished
off (but not yet!), burnished veterans gilded by loss
who glint like old bowling trophies in the right light.
Extinguishment is still far away we repeat under
our breaths at bedtime, like children who can't
remember their prayers. Come morning we'll step
out for a meatloaf sandwich (one our grown son
dubbed *meat-load* sandwich back when he was a ticklish
kid squishing it flat with his little hand so it'd fit into
his mouth). A humble dish with radish garnish,
it gives sagging spirits a lift and beguiles our tongues
with onions, mustard, and mortal sweetness welling
up from deep in the beef, which, if meat could speak
might moo or sigh: *Yes, I too was well fed in my time.*

Wanda Coleman

Unspoiled

After S. Teresa Piedra

these wounds return like old lovers

shadow scars deepen to red violet
as if merely stored in the flesh beneath.
i moan loudly in this sleepwalk, burns,
stingings & welts leeched into consciousness

as familiar as mother's beatings with belts, fists,
and switches—the epithets and manglings of my name

that peculiar song sung by one enraged: *would you like a spanking?*

erupts in my ears, upsets my stomach
rumbles in my bones and bowels

what have i done? i asked you then as ever i ask myself
your eyes answered and answer still: *you were born*

you nappy-headed bitch

the child i was adores you and despairs—for all time.
but for today's mean loneliness your scion loathes you

looking at my hands, identical to yours,
i see me slapping myself—the force of blows
knocks me back, across the decades, to my knees

where i cry "Daddy!" but he is seldom home

(the spankings stopped when i turned thirteen,
when i outgrew you and began my womanly bleeds
though the slaps continued)

now i will open my hand and heart
apply salve and solace. in these final days
grant myself breath
be the mother i deserved

Khaled Mattawa

The Violet Bends to the Stubble Skirting It

and the cat's head follows the arc of a sparrow's flight.
When you asked me "Are you sure you want to go?"
I said "no," and obeyed what I will never be able to name.
When I call out to you now
I still have to pause before calling her name,
and for endearments I have failed to tell you
anything other than what I've whispered to her.

But that's not why I'm not in love.

Once when I was ten I saw a neighbor
step out into a cold afternoon, shirtless.
He stood in front of his house, raised his arms
and yelled a triumphant cry. And as if to terrorize me
he let out a loud laugh.
He was the neighborhood "drinker"
reputed to sell the "grappa" he made in his garage.

Why am I telling you this
when all I want to say is that I'm not in love?

I sensed my terror and cradled it in the coat
I wrapped around me. But what am I cradling now
as I kiss you, as I caress your soft arms,
your hands fragile like sparrows
in my palms.

There are satisfactions beyond our reach.
We recognize them, envy them, and learn even to recoil from them.
Once in a friend's garden I had tea with three men.
The youngest among them spoke about an upcoming nephew's
    marriage they'd recently arranged.
He complimented the choice of bride and the new in-laws as being
    "like us,"
meaning modest, virtuous, reputable,
but so low-key that a scandal would not do them irreparable harm.
How can I describe that man's glee, his eyes two small flames
in the afternoon turning dusk, for he has now become an elder, young
    enough to facilitate the match and respected enough to object and
    be heard.

A breeze blows and the stubble sends the violet
a ruffian salute. The violet is unmoved,
but if you'd look closer it'd be easy to imagine
a tingling falling from its pistil to its thinnest root.
The cat watches like a Mafioso
with a developed taste for abstract art.

Sometimes I sit next to my mother in the large living room, and I can
    tell she is not there,
thinking of my father perhaps, or more likely thinking of her own
    death.
The last time I saw him alive she told me "it's as if he crawled out of a
    grave."
So many close calls had left us calloused,
but upon death a dizziness.
The so-much-still-to-do, the rug of one's life too far undone.
She sits there as if I am a distant light in her rear view mirror, and she
    driving on.
But I have nowhere to go, having come from so far away,
and having nothing to do there but to be her son.
So I begin to reel her in. I ask her to tell a story
and she takes that story as if she'd picked up a hitchhiker, glad for
    company and the purpose her new companion gives her.

Don't ask me what I'll do when that old woman dies. I can't bear the
    thought.

I think she thinks my father is now where he wants to be,
doing what he liked to do most,
which was work, and to fret about work,
seeking accolades he'd not gotten in earthly life,
never crying over spilt milk.
Muling. Bulldogging on.

Sometimes, I'd like to think that when she's deep in her telling, the
    hitchhiker she picks up bears the face of a man she loves,
and there they ride away into the dawn.

None of this has anything to do with you,
none of this has anything to do with having been burned by love or
    not wanting to be in love again.

When the drinker's wife knocked on our door one night,
my father answered.
He heard the woman out, but only offered to take her to the police.
Other neighbors took her in,
and because she was a foreigner, and because I knew what that meant
    even then,
I felt ashamed for her.
I never asked my father why he'd been so ungenerous because I
    thought one day I'd understand.

I still don't understand.

The man I spoke of earlier, whose life was beginning to ripen,
imagine him the same night he was engaged in matchmaking
    returning home to
the usual clutter of toys, the older boy not letting his younger brother
    have his turn at the PlayStation,
the toddler whimpering hanging on to his mother's dress,
    but she's cooking and has no time to carry him.
She shouts from inside the kitchen at her daughter, who has found a
    fondness for the telephone,
to pick up her baby brother and wash his face and take him to bed, but
    the girl pretends she hasn't heard,
and her mother shouts again this time threatening to smack her.

It's at this moment that the man enters his house, and he is quickly aware
that his girl is not being "a good older daughter,"
aware too that she's reached puberty, those tiny inflammations under her shirt,
which now makes him think that he needs to tell her mother that the girl must dress differently, no more jeans or tight shirts,
and he's also aware that she's a pretty girl, and in a few years
that will feel like a blink stinging his eyes, someone will come and ask for her hand.
Before saying hello he commands the girl to go to the kitchen and pick up the toddler,
he turns to the boys and asks if they'd done their homework,
and enters the kitchen—
his wife has never looked more beautiful to him,
and he has never been happier and suspects he may never be this happy again.

I know why I'm telling you about this man, and it will not surprise you.
When tragedy cannot slam her brakes in time,
when the light change heralds entrances into the self that keep shrinking . . .
It is a different story, nothing to do with not being in love.

When my father died, I knew exactly what I needed to do,
and saw myself filling the emptiness quickly with resolve,
my sharp edges rounding out.
It was an exhilarating feeling.
I was strangely in love with the world, ripe to be in love.

Then a few months later he began to reel me in, and I lay at his feet floundering.
He'd appear before me in the bed I saw him die in,
and as if on cue I'd begin to interrogate myself in his presence.
I could never tell if he wanted to forgive or be forgiven.
Even in sleep I rocked to his brutal wavering.

Listen, what can I weave when my hands keep slipping,
when the walls I touch bend with the force of anti-catharsis?

I think I hear a tune plucked on Oedipal chords.
I think I hear Hamlet dithering in his old age.
Must be the mood I'm in.
How else to brace you in your blooming, violet rising
among parched stubble in craggy fields?
That man is now a wet sparrow in the cold rain of widowhood,
his children more fragile than your hands,
and you so open and ready, wanting to love your life, to be surprised by
    your love for it,
leaning down on me, your weight doubled with joy, tripled with a
    ghost of despair.
I bend,
and I'm easily seducible because I'm not in love,
and you rise,
and you drift upward placing another brick at the top layer on the wall
    of your happy fortress.

Go ahead, I'll be your ladder again,
and this can go on for the rest of our lives,
but I'm not climbing along.
I'm not in love.

Cynie Cory

My Frigidaire

Forget the aftermath it's dead—
Your voice in the atomic room shifts
without a hint. Air
splits—I don't care, you lose,
broken hero, existential zero.
It's three degrees inside the Frigidaire.

I'm swallowing the rerun, (a gun's inside the Frigidaire).
There's a way, I don't know to show up dead
as a dog. I bury day in zero
the way minimum wage explains the shifts
that bone us. O story of how we lose!
The end of sight. My kiss nicks air.

What act is right when we're OFF-THE-AIR?
All-night symptomatic Frigidaire,
the comic quote unwinds. Hey! Last-to-Lose,
is loss the same? I can tell you I am dead
trembling tired, double-guessing, undressing in shifts.
No more universe to name. It's down to zero.

Come now, let's just—listen. What matters here is—Zero.
Foot in the door, crack it. You're repetitious as the air
that leaks from your Auto Discount tire that you won't fix. It shifts—
always—the conversation, every time the Frigidaire
hisses there's something missing, a comma or dead
regrets. It's all been said, she said. I don't want to lose

this—us—her. [Terrible line. (What to say) to lose
the past but gain the rent.] It's sub-zero,
uranium spent. Absence from absence is absence dead.
Trigger, you lover, you silent partner, tear the air
from dust. It's clear beyond us. I can't repair the Frigidaire. . . .
What song lifts toward the minioned dawn, what longing shifts

from here to here, the television-glare lisps, the image shifts
to black & white. There's no reason to fight or lose
the Lorazepam in my lap. Moreover, my Frigidaire
is poised to hum inside the room gone black as zero.
—A winter field iced in air—
O pharmacy of sky, don't disappear. I fear the dead.

If it were only half past zero
I could lay your head to the earnest air.
The way to lose the Frigidaire, shifts across what once was me, is dead.

Joyelle McSweeney

Septina

This is where the magic happens, and this is where I make my jams:
on the Lil' Marvel, with a turtlenecked lesbian forema, a quart of
    scotch bonnet,
a quart jar of scotch, rotten blueberries smashed like meth-mouth
    forgotten in their carton.
Outside a quantity of Maine rips off the line and flaps like Robert
    Lowell on a bender to land amid the low rocks in the bay.
    Ambitious tumblers
escort wide quantities of rum, lime juice, ice, and simple
syrup through the complicating hours of the day.

A string of mintleaves over the private hours of the day.
I mean the parts called *private* by the guards who cold wire the man by
    his joints to the jamb
like a lamb, and his guards are also called *private* though none of these
    any longer are. Nothing's simple
as this degraded square of photograph, her G.I. greens, his "restraint
    bonnet."
It points portentously, and then it lists. From Breton maids, bonnets
    rise like doves or tumblers
on an unseen wind that will blow them up (to heaven) through the
    tops of their heads like poems or suicide bombers. Light as meringue
    or the paper collar of a Corona or the 12-pack carton
of Corona Robert Lowell lifts right now to Madre Maria from the
    depths of his sort of Catholic soul/ bender.

He's a Yankee Catholic Confederate. Or now he's a Beat. As all time
    zones are the same to God, Who loves us Eastern, Central, and
    particularly Mountain, where, on the public access line, DJ Denver

answers questions from the unborn-again about black platter-shaped
   universes spinning backwards towards the big bang of the first day,
when God said the word and light poured down like smokes from the
   carton.
In the same breath, He sets his oil well on fire. He oils the jambs
and the axels so they all fall open towards catastrophe. The human
   race like plastic-monkey tumblers
shall be packed back into their toxic barrel and destroyed. Nothing
   could be simpler
than undoing this species that wants to hold on to flesh like a pathetic
   flea, black bonnet

of its carapace popped under a thumbnail's pressure. Life reversible as a
   metaphor. On the bonnet
of the Astin-Martin, a Michangelic fresco of lost insectoidal life. For
   the night cometh when no man can go on a bender
or go back and add two commas to that sentence where the phrase
   could be hypothetically excised or simply
left out altogether. That phrase being your life. As days left out
   overnight turn pale with moisture, as days
roll back like eyes, tumblers
shake in the lock of life like paper tigers. The gate rattles open. The
   enjambed

centuries tip; the oil lamps flare; boxes of manuscripts and booze and
   conflagrating curtains and couches jam
the ether already ashy with smokers' breath, cat-gut, whalebone
   buttons, bon mots,
the hair where venom is stored and soft-tissue where memory is stored,
   the cartons
of Super 8's where memory is stored and typewriters with jammed
   returns are stored and schooldays bent
over nailed-down desks of memory the boy stood in the burning
   schoolroom with the enemy combatant for whom the ash rises from
   the world like tumblers
from the circus net, as was foretold in the second stanza, if it were not
   so, I would have told you, rises like the ringing of a bell, to the
   simple
world of day without days,

maybe, Amen. All boiling down to a burnt and sour-sweet jam, a
   greengage,
a glass bonnet with a stern judgmental lever on it
snapped mightily into place. Carton bender simple tumbler day

James Hall

Portrait of My Lover Singing in Traffic

Man rushing onto Sunrise Boulevard, singing Disorder
in the Flesh: first threadbare notes, then his trousers

stunning the air—man singing the Jackknifed Torso,
Stabbed Back songs, man jerking between rows of cars,

people locking their doors, their faces ashen when at last
his shirt comes off. Wind carrying the ripped bar

of fabric to the sidewalk where I catch him, fitting fingers
to places his skin had been. Man rushing into traffic

losing his shoes, their holes like something singed.
Then his underwear. Then he's naked, I Ain't Got No Body.

Everyone watching, moving their lips, the train guards
lowering the song of the mechanical flashing arm,

stopping all of us. The muscle of him unstoppable,
uncontrollable song. Sirens reddening air,

a mouth opening back the counterweight song, I Been Rent
By Tougher Men, which becomes so quickly the Gravelmouth,

the Spreadleg, the Ribkicked song, which gives way behind glass
in the police cruiser to the I've Been Your Bulletproof

Piece of Ass, Now Take Me to Where I'll Die
in Shadow song. Inside my shattershot skin I sing

the broken ballads my mother taught me: My Body Severed
in Fogsway, the Derailed Train is My Shepherd

I Shall Not Want, her voice audible even under all that
copmuscle and metal, singing the Song of Stained

and Never More Beautiful Than Criminal, and the man
is my mother, I'm filled with want. The lyrics are rushing

unbidden out of me, joining the shirtless choir in the street,
all hands locking, webbed behind the head, face between the legs

kicked apart, singing Don't Grieve So Open,
in motherless tones, right on through from the beginning.

A Fact Which Occurred in America

In the fifth grade, when we came finally to the Civil
War, the teacher kept saying over and over *We lost,*
we lost, his eyes a shadowy grief under his favorite painting,

a laminated Dawe reproduction subtitled *A fact which occurred*
in America: a Black man wrestling a buffalo to the ground.
The ground becomes his grave, I am the buffalo.

In the painting of the buffalo rolling his eye
to size up the man who will never be strong enough
to wrestle his way out of the definition of black,

I am trying to say *we are metaphors for each other, please*
don't kill me. The man is black but so is the buffalo,
so is the sky and so is the heart which keeps this fact holy.

In the painting I am the buffalo because I want to be loved
by pure physicality, a man with broad hips and broader anger
and a yoke around his neck which has not broken him yet.

In the painting about a buffalo's last breath, I am the dust
matted on the lips, desire's last yoke. Kiss me, keep me
in your mouth, don't let me dissolve into fact.

In the painting about a boy who writes *I am sorry we lost*
the Civil War fifty times on the blackboard after school
in his deserted fifth grade class, I am the bone-white chalk,

I have always wanted to be someone's defiled good buffalo.
In the painting the man tells the buffalo, *play dead,*
I'll get you out of this. In the defiled fifth-grade teacher's

laminated copy of the painting, I am the racing pulse
of the boy getting his revenge when the teacher isn't looking.
I am the time after we learned about the heroic Civil War,

on the playground when Day-Trion caught me alone
in the maze of trees and held me down with one hand,
kissed me with his tongue, licking my lip first, smoothing it

for his, my first kiss, on the ground, the leaves widening
under us, black and wet. Deep in the animal-wrestled-down
part of me, the boy was bent like a tree over a maze

scribbling a hyphenated name in tiny scrawl in black ink
on a piece of paper, trying all hour during language arts
to get back to the maze when the teacher snatches up the paper,

his eyes widening, recognizing the beginning of darker revolt.
In the punishment, I was the blackboard, my body
lashed by loss and sorrow. I was the buffalo,

I wanted to lose the war, I wanted to stay black,
the filmy white chalk a sickness stretched over my skin.
In that America, I am always betraying the master.

Tom C. Hunley

Musives and a Silent Crump

Musive was a fine word, the name of a moth, gone extinct.
Crump: the sound of a heavy shell or bomb. *Hurkle:* a crouching,
cowering motion. *Erump:* to erupt, burst forth. Were these words
phased out, slow, or did they surface and then disappear,
shy as whale backs? Maybe they entered and exited the language
in a rush, like *groovy*, *rad*, and *word up*, slang terms teens use,
then don't use, like hangouts turned "wack"
by the sudden arrival of parents. So many words,
but none for the smiles that flickered from Jane to me,

and back, when we'd reached a place in our life together
where we almost didn't need words. No word for
the strange joy I felt, cutting our firstborn son's umbilical cord
as he lay screaming on Jane's stomach. So many words,
but none tickled our infant son's throat.
Jane and I came to understand, this cry meant *I'm hungry*,
that one meant *burp me*, another meant *change me*.
Italians have seven words for "the," so why can't we
have words that distinguish a baby's different types of tears,

or a special word for the tears on Jane's face as she dug
her fingernails into her cheeks after he died in his crib?
Have you ever scratched someone, by accident,
as your arms grazed? I know the word for that. It's *scrazing*,
but I had no words to comfort Jane. *I'm sorry. It'll be okay.*
I knew these words didn't mean as much as I needed them to.
I had no words for the beasts eating my insides, musives
in a trunk full of clothes, no words for the hole I felt
and tried to fill with my writing, with my music,

with Camels and Jim Beam. And when Jane sought comfort
in another man's arms, when I found a red strand
of that man's hair on my pillow, on my bed,
when I was forced to imagine their wordless moans,
a silent crump shocked my senses, left me hurkling, unable to erump.
The words *cuckold* and *how could you?* and *I'll kill him!*
weren't there for me. *Wife* and *son* had turned into archaisms.
I had nothing but my dictionary, which grunted, sighed, and shrugged,
a friend who had no words that could comfort me.

Jill Drumm

Ode to My Pantry

Whatever God-poke people get in church or frisson of allegiance
    sports fans
        tap into during opening anthems, gets me all aplotz
when I behold your cornucopian larder, O repository of all urges
    theurgic
        and arsenal of prandial hocus-pocus
harbingered by your Madagscar vanilla, raspberry blush vinegar,
        unleavened prawn crackers, ungrated nutmegs, arachnid legs
of Spanish saffron threads—holy-holy men in saffron-dyed robes,
        225,000 plucked stigmas of *Crocus sativus* adding up to a
           grocer's pound,
so precious that the natal triumvirate could have blown in
    with gifts of frankincense, saffron, and myrrh.

Reliquary of five-course zealotry with your back rows
    and high-shelf pecking order of the subordinates
like rose water extract, anise seeds, buckwheat flour, mung bean threads,
    and segregated Caro Syrups, light and dark,
narthexed like tertiary members of the congregation
    of the Holy Roller Tabernacle of Betty Crocker in San Crisco,
shrine of Saints Jemima and Godiva,
    attended by Father McCormick, Brother Smucker,
and Sisters SueBee and Luzianne.
    There's the hermetic ruby tins of smoked Atlantic oysters
stacked like uncut Hoyle decks, and cubed lamés of chicken-yellow
    bouillon.
    O the soupçon god-wrath of wasabi powder and brittle
        festoons
of cellophaned noodles poised for unraveling in the boiling pot,

and quills of rosemary resinous and heady as a Douglas fir
just shivered in through the front door—
        the one unflagging Christmas joy left
after shuffling between dad's undecorated house,
        with maybe a parchy poinsettia that sprouted sappy milk
from the joints of its involucral bracts if you tortured the leaves—
        and Mom's house, all done up in high kitsch with papier-
                mâché
and rococo gilds of dried macaroni tableaus, a vertiginous glitter
        of construction-paper chains wafty in the bronchial blasts
of central heat denuding the pine tree way before December twenty-
    fifth;

        daily nose-bleed dry air, explaining why I associate bloody
                noses
with those piquant cinnamon red-hots used on holiday cookies
        the angels' rubicund bug-eyes bugging me
with their Amityville connotations,
        not unlike the odium reserved for the bloated reindeer
waddling in formation out of the oven, so globulous
        that no amount of colored-sugar virtuosity
could make them resemble anything so much as
        well-fed collies with cosmically-attuned headgear,
And the nose-bleeds!
        Caused by dessicated mucosa or hormonal vacillations,
so at thirteen I would get one with every period,
        prompting Mom's horrific joke about bleeding from both
                ends—
what was she thinking? and then I read in Freud's Interpretation of
    Dreams
        that they were a symptom of his hysterical female patients,
like the famous Dora, I think was her name, but that word hysterical
        made me worry, with good cause, in secret.

Jeez, the secrets you pantries keep! The ideal locus, really,
        with your take-that-Freudian goblin markets
of plus ça change satisfactions and oblique come-hithers:
        the pantry's always open, honey, come on inside for a little
                Southern Comfort;
and all your sacred collaborations toward

the gobbledygook perfume of dried garlic, orange extract,
and fuzzy rings of maple syrup gathering mysteriously
    like the caked-flour and molasses-goo divots
in the terra incognita of every pantry I've ever had.
    Sometimes all I have to do is open your door, and inspiration
sprouts like the spring-green stubble erupted from onions going soft.
    I no longer rely on the grease-worn and egg-spackled recipe
        cards
once guarded like a tarot pack, or invoke the elder culinary wizards
    as I pore over *Fannie Farmer* or *Southern Living*
with its pages stuck together from that gingerbread waffle accident,
    so chapter three (Breads)
is pintoed with pumpkinesque stains, gummy

    like the hand mixer my mom used and I think rarely wiped
        clean,
but I still have this relic and won't throw it away, despite the time
    it fell into the dishwater and I prayed I had it right when I
        pulled the plug
before plunging my hand into the suds to retrieve it.
    I like to think some of her boiled frosting or Tollhouse
        molecules
still linger in the mixer's crevices, a blessing as I approach your late-
    night closet
    of neo-magus concoctions, guided by the litany
of my sins and successes and the protean inventory of your shelves
    cosmically fillable with the mystery of zero's plenitude,
and other times bare as the hope
    that I will ever achieve the pinnacle of my mother's banana
        cake
or emerge transformed by your phone booth-sized darkness
    as the daughter who will save her.

David Graham

Between Classes

> There's nothing worse than old people talking about sex.
> Student, overheard in the hallway

Nothing worse than your lumpy baggage,
flabby duffels and bulging roll-ons
with burst seams and scuffed straps, passports
all smudged with vanished holiday.

Nothing worse than being crisscrossed
with scars you see and those you don't,
some moss-eyed gargoyle in the mirror
having so little to do
with your former cool stream self.

So cover your love with cloudy comforter,
turn the dark down a few notches,
and be quiet about it, please—nothing worse
than those baby sounds from your throats
taking animal pleasure from time.

How dare you strut that mothball stuff
across our dance floor—don't you know
why your babies' tongues are pierced?
Can't you read the ink on our icebright skin?

No one wants the blood lecture,
the arid anecdote. Don't you remember
this radiator hiss of wisdom
in dusty afternoon? Nothing sadder

than a wrinkled hipster, still groping
the lingo hopefully, fingering the clothes,
doing that clunk-kneed cha-cha in full view.

Don't be spilling your mess of coffee grounds
and apple peels in *our* sun. . . . You should
practice safe sex, Sir, in the dumpster
of your mind, all overripe with vocabulary.

Opening Credits

Six A.M., seven—it's summer so I can slowly watch
the day begin, settling back into my pillow as if
that new movie I've been hearing so much about
is just now running its opening credits,
names of excellent quirky under-recognized actors
scrolling across blue sky and yard oaks
with their skittery fresh leaves, and a subtle form
of melody in the May air, something so delicately
composed you barely hear it, just feel this overwhelming
anticipation, curiosity not just about the day
with its Cheerios and quite decent pot
of Colombian coffee but really the whole magilla,
the dappled fevery agile world flexing its sexy thighs,
tossing its hair in the bug-free breeze

—I know this coming day will ripen with possibility,
solid real complications, not like Hollywood, not
wavebreaking tumult or glamorous goo
with wind machines and hysterical John Williams score
but an indie flick sort of kitchen clutter all so meaningful
and tender in its true handheld essence,
with half-eaten eggs congealing on a plate, yes exactly!

and a woman in her bathrobe that looks precisely
as her bathrobe would look sits at the table
in front of those fried eggs, not making a big deal
out of anything, especially not her quite lovely thighs
emerging under that poorly lit table
—poorly lit for no reason! this isn't set design! It's life!—

and she is doing the crossword, as it happens,
maybe completely ignoring the day's dawning news,
or maybe she's read it already, as much of those
hopeless headlines as she cares to—the point is,
it doesn't matter, it's just achingly germane to see
how she stops eating her eggs, she's full now,

and there are of course those five pounds she's been
meaning to take off anyway, notwithstanding

she looks pretty terrific to any honest eye
in her ten year old bathrobe and just-washed hair,
no makeup for God's sake, this is *real*,
remember?—so when I walk into the kitchen
completely without twinkly Tom Cruise strut
and devoid even of Jack Nicholson balding charisma,

just amble in with my mug of cooling coffee
to see what's what, this truly compelling woman,
very alluring in her offbeat no-bullshit kind of way
and, as later developments will make very clear,
a truly intelligent multi-layered flawed funny
lovely character, this woman whose mere name
on the video box will make me smile, looks up
in that perfectly straight way she has and asks me
for a six-letter word meaning "to feather an arrow,"
and though I admit I don't have it on the tip
of my tongue, yes it takes me a couple guesses, in fact,
pretty soon I am able to nail it ("fledge")
just the way she suspected I would—well, in case
you're wondering, that's the kind of day this is.

Recycled Air

Essay on poetics

Count me fascinated but wary, I guess you could say,
with all these loopy self-reflexive poems I'm seeing lately,
running my finger down the insouciant spines at Borders or Barnes &
    Noble,
all of us basking in the scent of Colombian coffee
and ridiculous millennial prosperity—O apolitical self-absorbed
    solidarity,
O poets like David Lehman and Denise Duhamel and Mark Halliday,
Campbell McGrath or the latest Billy Collins saxophone solo running
    the changes
of its own leafy, air-filled composition out under the minor-key maples,
and naturally John Ashbery when he isn't being entirely vaporous,
and Kenneth Koch granddaddy of it all, that perpetual Terrible Child,
who was armored even into his 70s in those trademark titanium
    whimsies,
no Yeatsean gongs or goose-flock fanfares for him, nosiree,
always a moving target, always quite the surprise-meister in his motley
    glide
over the thin ice of rapidly encroaching mortality—

You see the sort of poem I mean, a talky loose-lined ramble
that can embrace actual names and trivia (Kenneth's iron hair
and gaze of melting cheese, Billy's spit valve, Denise's private thoughts
hurled to the sands of time like vile underwear at a nude beach)
a poem that can even absorb portentous jabs
like "rapidly encroaching mortality," all the while dithering
over its own ongoing revisions, its squalid flaws and delusions
(would "rapidly enclosing" be better, do you think?) all
enjoyed—to be quite honest about it—like fart bubbles in the bath.

The point, I suppose, is to charm everyone with your winking
self-enclosure, to say yes I know my own tin-can absurdity
even better than you do, Gentle Reader, and isn't it fun
to put aside for a few hours at least all the ponderous theories

and monkey-chatter voices that say a poem (or life) should should
   should?
Not that there isn't ample precedent, said the Professor: remember
Whitman's cheery warning that "querilities, / Ungracious glooms,
   aches,
lethargy, constipation, whimpering ennui / May filter in my daily
   songs"?
Do I test your patience with my po-mo yawp? Very well then,
I test your patience with my insufferable po-mo yawp. So sue me. . . .

And just when you think the poem's going to spin out utterly
into neurotic self-analysis or surreal gloop gloop,
why that's precisely when the poet spins a gosh-darn good yarn
(examples fail me at the moment, but you can imagine, can't you?)
or works in a moving quote from Neruda, or maybe an allusion
to Roland Barthes that beyond the drippy sarcasm of its placement
signals hey! this poet's no dum-dum, and even when veering
deep into the wilds of the Home Shopping Network
there seems some ultimate seriousness afoot, however silly
or mock-agonized, and just then upon the burning sands
of that selfsame nude beach will appear a Venus or Apollo
of throat-catching unironized beauty—
so that turns out to be the poem's final secret, that it's none other
than our old friend Mr. Lyric Eye doing lines on the mirror,
licking his (or her!) sorry salted wounds again,
not at all the glinting postmodern riff we thought.

Or maybe it is. So hard to tell, for now the poem
will swerve again, offering a few strident remarks about
the classbound assumptions of such *poesis* in the twilight
of the implosion of late capitalism, which will be
deliberately difficult to disentangle from the paraphrased
plot of an obscure Steve McQueen flick or some apparently
good advice on the best way to cook mushrooms

or—well, you get the point, don't you? You you you
my oh-so-acute longsuffering and canny reader, in fact
secretly one of my biggest admirers, though you're too skittery
to send me that fan letter you've often contemplated—afraid that
my Kevlar-vest ironies would deflect it like nothing, and there you'd be,

feeling like some eternal sophomore instead of what you are,
my camarado, my chum, my peer in this difficult peerless art,
a poet just on the verge of major recognition yourself,
as anyone can see who's read your poems, which of course I have,
I'm your greatest promoter, which you in turn have surely guessed,
having purchased all my hard to find chapbooks and looked me up
on the web, too, carefully distinguishing me from David Graham
the famous though over-the-hill golfer, Davy Graham
the ace British folk guitarist, David Graham the mystery novelist,
David Graham the Canadian French scholar, and David Graham
the kitsch photographer—who by the way never returned
my earnest fan letter, thus dashing my hopes of a collaboration,
the beauteous thought of a coffee table book with poems
by David Graham illustrated by David Graham, with perhaps
an introduction (what the hey) by my nephew (David Graham). . . .

Well, anyway, before this turns into a canto or something
let's join hands now and wade into history soup together
wearing our Truth Is Beauty bathing suits (or not! cast off your
outmoded solemnities! Don't sweat the small stuff!)
and above all a knowing sort of K-Mart Frank O'Hara smile.
That's Francis P. O'Hara, by the way, my ice-fishing neighbor,
not the poet you're thinking of, the one who in point of fact *invented*
insouciance in a Soho bar in 1949 and then left it
(generous man!) lying about for just anyone to use . . .

CONTRIBUTORS

Kim Addonizio's most recent book is *Little Beauties: A Novel* (Simon & Schuster, 2005). She is also the author of several collections of poetry, including *What Is This Thing Called Love* and *Tell Me*, which was a finalist for the 2000 National Book Award. **Dick Allen** is the author of seven collections of poetry, including *The Day Before: New Poems* (Sarabande, 2003), winner of the Sheila Motion Poetry Award, and *Ode to the Cold War: Poems New and Selected* (Sarabande Books, 1997). He has poems recently published or forthcoming in the *Atlantic Monthly*, the *Ontario Review*, the *Hudson Review*, the *Nation*, the *North American Review*, the *New Criteron*, and *Salmagundi*. His work is included in five editions of *The Best American Poetry*. **Nin Andrews**'s next book, *Sleeping With Houdini*, is forthcoming from BOA Editions. **Polina Barskova** was born in Petersburg, Russia. She is the author of six books of poetry in Russian and professor of Russian literature at Hampshire College. **Josh Bell**'s first book is *No Planets Strike* (University of Nebraska, 2004). He is currently a Ph.D candidate at the University of Cincinnati. **Margaret Benbow**'s first collection, *Stalking Joy* (Texas Tech University Press, 1997), won the Walt McDonald First Book Award. She has just completed a second collection, *Sight to Behold*. Her

story "Boy into Panther" may be read on the *Zoetrope: All Story* site. **Adrian Blevins** is the author of *The Brass Girl Brouhaha* (Ausable Press, 2003) and *The Man Who Went Out for Cigarettes* (Small Press Distribution, 1996). She teaches at Roanoke College in Salem, Virginia. **Daniel Borzutzky** is the author of *Arbitrary Tales* (Triple Press, 2005) and *The Ecstacy of Capitulation* (BlazeVox Books, 2007). His translation of the work of Chilean poet Jaime Luis Huenun will be published in 2007 by Action Books. **Catherine Bowman** is the author of *Notarikon* (Four Way Books, 2006), *Rock Farm* (Gibbs Smith, 1996), *1-800-Hot-Ribs* (Gibbs Smith, 1993) and the editor of *Word of Mouth: Poems Featured On NPR's All Things Considered* (Vintage, 2003). She is the Ruth Lilly Professor of Poetry at Indiana University. Her collection of poems on Sylvia Plath, *The Plath Cabinet*, is forthcoming from Four Way Books in 2007. **Jason Bredle** is the author of *A Twelve Step Guide* (New Michigan, 2004) and *Standing In Line for the Beast* (New Issues, 2007). Winner of the 2004 New Michigan Press Chapbook Contest and the 2006 New Issues Poetry Prize, he lives in Chicago. **Cathleen Calbert** is the author of two books of poetry, *Lessons in Space* (University of Florida Press, 1997) and *Bad Judgment* (Sarabande Books, 1998). Her third collection of poems, *Sleeping with a Famous Poet*, is forthcoming in 2007 (CustomWords, WordTech Communications). She is professor of English at Rhode Island College, where she directs the creative writing program. **Richard Cecil** is the author of four collections of poetry, most recently *Twenty-First Century Blues* (Southern Illinois University Press, 2004). He teaches at Indiana University in Bloomington and in the brief residency MFA program at Spalding University. **David Clewell** has published six collections of poems, most recently *The Low End of Higher Things* (University of Wisconsin Press, 2003) and two book-length poems, *The Conspiracy Quartet* and *Jack Ruby's America* (Garlic Press, 1997 and 2000). He teaches at Webster University in St. Louis. **Wanda Coleman** received the 1999 Lenore Marshall Poetry Prize (*Bathwater Wine*) and was nominated for the 2001 National Book Award (*Mercurochrome*). Her new books include *Ostinato Vamps, Wanda Coleman: Greatest Hits 1966-2003,* and *The Riot Inside Me: More Trials & Tremors.* **Billy Collins**'s latest collection is *The Trouble With Poetry and Other Poems* (Random House, 2005). **Cynie Cory** is the author of *American Girl* (New Issues, 2007). **Carl Dennis**'s latest collection of poetry is *Unknown Friends* (Penguin, 2007). In 2002, he received a Pulitzer for *Practical Gods* (Penguin, 2001). **Gregory Djanikian** is the author of four collections of poetry, most recently, *Years Later* (Carnegie Mellon University Press, 2000). His new collection, *So I Will Till the Ground,* also from Carnegie Mellon, is forthcoming in 2007. He directs the creative writing program at the University of Pennsylvania. **Stephen Dobyns**'s most recent book of poems is *Mystery, So Long* (Penguin, 2005). **Jill Drumm** received her MFA in Creative Writing from Florida International University, where she was the executive editor of *Golf Stream* magazine.

In 2006, she received an Academy of American Poets Prize. **Denise Duhamel**'s most recent collections are *Two and Two* (University of Pittsburgh Press, 2005), *Mille et un sentiments* (Firewheel Editions, 2005), and *Queen for a Day: Selected and New Poems* (University of Pittsburgh Press, 2001). **Stephen Dunn** is the author of thirteen collections of poetry, including the recently published *Everything Else in the World* (W.W. Norton & Co.). He was awarded the Pulitzer Prize for *Different Hours* in 2001. **B. H. Fairchild** is the recipient of Guggenheim, Rockefeller, and NEA fellowships. His most recent book of poems is *Local Knowledge* (W. W. Norton & Co., 2005). **Steve Fellner**'s first book of poems, *Blind Date with Cavafy,* will be published by Marsh Hawk Press in 2007. He currently teaches at SUNY Brockport. **Amy Gerstler**'s most recent books of poetry include *Ghost Girl* (2004), *Medicine* (2000), and *Crown of Weeds* (1997), all published by Penguin. She teaches in the Bennington Writing Seminars Program at Bennington College in Vermont and at Art Center College of Design in Pasadena, California. **Albert Goldbarth**'s most recent book is *The Kitchen Sink: New and Selected Poems 1972-2007* (Graywolf Press, 2007). **David Graham**'s books of poetry include *Second Wind* (Texas Tech, 1990) and *Stutter Monk* (Flame Press, 2000). He is the co-editor, with Kate Sontas, of the essay anthology *After Confession* (Graywolf, 2001) and professor of English at Ripon College. **Gabriel Gudding** is the author of two books, *A Defense of Poetry* (Pitt Poetry Series, 2002) and *rhode island notebook,* forthcoming from Dalkey

Archive Press in 2008. He teaches literature and creative writing at Illinois State University. **James Hall** is assistant professor of English at Bethany College. He holds a Ph.D from the University of Houston and an MFA from Bennington. **Mark Halliday**'s four books of poems are *Little Star* (William Morrow, 1987), *Tasker Street* (University of Massachusetts, 1992), *Selfwolf* (University of Chicago, 1999), and *Jab* (University of Chicago, 2002). **Barbara Hamby**'s third book of poems is *Babel* (University of Pittsburgh Press, 2004). Her poems have recently appeared in *Ploughshares*, the *Yale Review*, and the *Paris Review*. She teaches in the creative writing department at Florida State University. **Bob Hicok**'s fifth book, *This Clumsy Living*, will be out from Pitt in Spring 2007. **Tony Hoagland** won the 2005 Mark Twain Award from the Poetry Foundation. A book of craft essays, *Real Sofistikashun*, will be out in October from Graywolf Press. He teaches at the University of Houston and in the Warren Wilson MFA Program. **Richard Howard**'s latest book is *The Silent Treatment* (Turtle Point Press 2005). He teaches at Columbia University's School of the Arts (Writing Division). Andrew Hudgins is the author of several books of poetry, including *Ecstatic in the Poison* (Overlook Press, 2003) and *Babylon in a Jar: Poems* (Mariner Books, 1998). **Tom C. Hunley** is assistant professor of English at Western Kentucky University and the director of Steel Toe Books (*www.steeltoebooks.com*). His books include *The Tongue* (Wind, 2004), *Still, There's a Glimmer* (WordTech, 2004), *My Life as a Minor Character* (Pecan Grove,

2005), and *Teaching Poetry Writing: A Five Canon Approach* (Multilingual Matters, 2007). **Roy Jacobstein**'s *A Form of Optimism* (University Press of New England, 2006) won the Samuel French Morse Prize, selected by Lucia Perillo. His previous book, *Ripe* (University of Wisconsin Press, 2002), won the Felix Pollak Prize. His poetry is included in *Literature: Reading Fiction, Poetry & Drama* (McGraw-Hill, 2006). He is an international public health physician. **Rodney Jones**'s eighth poetry collection, *Salvation Blues: 100 Poems, 1985-2005*, was recently published by Houghton Mifflin. **David Kirby** is the Robert O. Lawton Distinguished Professor of English at Florida State University and the author most recently of *The Ha-Ha*. **Caroline Knox**'s collection *He Paves the Road with Iron Bars* (Verse Press, 2004) won the 2005 Maurice English Award. She has recent work in Boston Review and Yale Review and is completing a sixth collection, *Quaker Guns*, forthcoming from Wave Books. **Dorianne Laux**'s fourth book of poems, *Facts About the Moon*, was published by W. W. Norton & Co. in 2005. **Cecilia Llompart** is currently an undergraduate Creative Writing major at the Florida State University. Her "revision" of the Lord's Prayer has received awards from Florida State's Department of English, as well as the American Academy of Poets. **Adrian C. Louis** teaches in the Minnesota State University System. His most recent book of poems is *Evil Corn* (Ellis Press, 2004). **Thomas Lux**'s most recent book is *The Cradle Palace* (Houghton Mifflin, 2004). **Jynne Dilling Martin** works at Random House and has her MFA from Warren Wilson. Her poems have recently appeared in the *Kenyon Review*. She lives in New York City with her husband and cat. **Cate Marvin**'s second book of poems, *Fragments of the Head of a Queen*, will be published by Sarabande Books in 2007. She is associate professor of creative writing at the College of Staten Island, City University of New York. **Khaled Mattawa** is the author of *Zodiac of Echoes* (Ausable Press, 2003) and *Ismailia Eclipse* (Sheep Meadow Press, 1995) and has translated several books of contemporary Arabic poetry. **Campbell McGrath** most recent book of poems is *Pax Atomica* (Ecco Press, 2005). He teaches at Florida International University in Miami. **Joyelle McSweeney** is the author of *The Commandrine & Other Poems* and *The Redbird*, both from Fence, and the novella, *Nylund, the Sarcographer*, forthcoming from Tarpulin Sky. She is a co-founder of Action Books and teaches in the MFA program at Notre Dame. **Joseph Millar**'s poems have appeared in *New Letters, Ploughshares, DoubleTake, Manoa,* and *Shenandoah*. His first book, *Overtime*, was a finalist for the Oregon Book Award. A new collection, *Fortune,* is out from Eastern Washington University Press. He teaches in Pacific University's low residency MFA and at Oregon State University. **Phyllis Moore**'s book of stories, *A Compendium of Skirts*, was published by Carroll and Graf in 2002. She is the director of Liberal Studies at the Kansas City Art Institute. **Aimee Nezhukumatathil** is the author of *Miracle Fruit* and *At the Drive-In Volcano* (both from Tupelo Press). New work appears in *Crazyhorse, Tin House,* and *Prairie Schooner*. She is associate professor of English at SUNY-Fredonia. **Sharon Olds** is working on her ninth book of poems, *O Western Wind*. **Danielle Pafunda** is author of *Pretty Young Thing* (Soft Skull Press, 2005). Her poetry and reviews appear in such publications as *Best American Poetry* (2006 and 2004), *Conjunctions, The Georgia Review,* and *Jubilat*. She is co-editor of the online journal *La Petite Zine*, and currently lives in Athens, Georgia. **Lucia Perillo**'s new book is *Luck Is Luck* (Random House, 2005). She lives in Olympia, Washington. **Lawrence Raab** is the author of six collections of poems, including *What We Don't Know About Each Other* (winner of the National Poetry Series and a finalist for the 1993 National Book Award), *The Probable World* (2000), and most recently *Visible Signs: New and Selected Poems* (2003), all published by Penguin. He teaches literature and writing at Williams College. **Natasha Rocas** lives in Tallahassee, FL, where she is studying creative writing at Florida State University. **John Rybicki**'s latest collection, *We Bed Down into Water: Poems,* is forthcoming from Triquarterly Books/Northwestern University Press in 2008. He is also the author of *Yellow-Haired Girl with Spider* (March Street Press, 2002) and *Traveling at High Speeds* (New Issues Poetry Press, 1996). **Steve Scafidi** is a cabinetmaker and lives with his family in West Virginia. He is the author of *Sparks from a Nine-Pound Hammer* (2001) and *For Love of Common Words* (2006), both from Louisiana State University Press. **Jon Schneider** graduated from Florida State

University and is currently attending the MFA program at the University of Virginia. **Martha Silano** has two full-length poetry collections, *Blue Positive* (Steel Toe, 2006) and *What the Truth Tastes Like* (Nightshade Press, 1999). **Gerald Stern** is the author of numerous collections of poetry, including *Everything is Burning* (2005), *American Sonnets* (2002), and *This Time: New and Selected Poems* (1998), which won the National Book Award all from W.W. Norton & Co. **Charles Harper Webb**'s book *Amplified Dog* (Red Hen Press, 2006) won the Saltman Prize for Poetry. *Hot Popsicles* was published in 2005 by the University of Wisconsin Press. Recipient of grants from the Whit-ing and Guggenheim Foundations, he directs creative writing at California State University, Long Beach. **Robert Wrigley** teaches at the University of Idaho. His most recent book is *Earthly Meditations: New and Selected Poems* (Penguin, 2006). **Susan Wood** is the author of three books of poems, most recently *Asunder* (Penguin, 2001), a National Poetry Series Winner. *Campo Santo* (Louisiana State University Press, 1991) won the Lamont Prize of the Academy of American Poets. She is the Gladys Louise Fox Professor of English at Rice University. **Dean Young**'s most recent book is *Embryoyo* (McSweeney's, 2007).

Subscriptions
Three issues per year. **Individuals:** one
year $24; two years $44; life $600. **Insti-
tutions:** one year $36; two years $68.
Overseas: $5 per year additional. Price
of back issues varies. Sample copies $5.
Address correspondence and subscriptions
to *TriQuarterly*, Northwestern University,
629 Noyes St., Evanston, IL 60208-4210.
Phone (847) 491-7614.

Submissions
The editors invite submissions of fiction,
poetry and literary essays, which must
be postmarked between October 1 and
March 31; manuscripts postmarked be-
tween April 1 and September 30 will
not be read. No manuscripts will be re-
turned unless accompanied by a stamped,
self-addressed envelope. All manuscripts
accepted for publication become the
property of *TriQuarterly*, unless other-
wise indicated.

Reprints
Reprints of issues 1–17 of *TriQuarterly*
are available in full format from Kraus
Reprint Company, Route 100, Millwood,
NY 10546, and all issues in microfilm
from University Microfilms International,
300 North Zeeb Road, Ann Arbor, MI
48106.

Indexing
TriQuarterly is indexed in the Humanities
Index (H. W. Wilson Co.), the American
Humanities Index (Whitson Publishing
Co.), Historical Abstracts, MLA, EBSCO
Publishing (Peabody, MA) and Informa-
tion Access Co. (Foster City, CA).

Distributors
Our national distributors to retail trade
are Ingram Periodicals (La Vergne, TN);
B. DeBoer (Nutley, NJ); Ubiquity (Brook-
lyn, NY); Armadillo (Los Angeles, CA).

Publication of *TriQuarterly* is made
possible in part by the donors of gifts
and grants to the magazine. For their
recent and continuing support, we are
very pleased to thank the Illinois Arts
Council, the Lannan Foundation, the
National Endowment for the Arts,
the Sara Lee Foundation, the Wendling
Foundation and individual donors.

RICHARD BAUSCH ANN BEATTIE GEORGE GARRETT
MADISON SMARTT BELL JOY WILLIAMS RICK BASS
FREDERICK BUSCH PAM DURBAN RON CARLSON
WILLIAM KITTREDGE LYNNE SHARON SCHWARTZ
PADGETT POWELL DORIS BETTS LEE K. ABBOTT
STUART DYBEK R. T. SMITH MELANIE RAE THON
EDITH PEARLMAN DAVID MADDEN CHRIS OFFUTT
CAROLYN COOKE JOHN KINSELLA DONALD HALL
STEPHEN DIXON CARY HOLLADAY DAVID HUDDLE
JENNIFER HAIGH TONY DOERR STEPHEN MINOT
GORDON WEAVER MICHAEL PARKER DAVE SMITH
ADAM DESNOYERS ALYSON HAGY JOAN CONNOR

The Idaho Review

Work from *The Idaho Review* has appeared in *The Best American Short Stories, Prize Stories: The O. Henry Awards, The Pushcart Prize: Best of the Small Presses,* and *New Stories from the South.*

Mitch Wieland, Editor
BOISE STATE UNIVERSITY 1910 UNIVERSITY DRIVE BOISE ID 83725